George the Orphan Crow
and the
Creatures of
Blossom Valley

Helen Fox

for my son Michael

George the Orphan Crow and the Creatures of Blossom Valley

One

The sun was heading towards the west when Plato, the old owl of Penny Wood, flew up on his tree. He stretched his legs, flexed his talons, and for a while sat basking in the glow of the setting sun. Then, in the peacefulness of Penny Wood he shut his eyes and nodded off.

Suddenly, a rumble broke out somewhere deep in the woods and was gradually coming closer. Plato didn't stir. He listened. The sound rumbled on at intervals and he knew what it was, for in his long life in Penny Wood he'd grown all too familiar with such sounds.

"Frenzied hunters," he moaned drowsily, then closed his eyes and drifted into a deep sleep.

***

A young crow and his parents sat close together, numbed with fear at the dreadful noise that was tearing through the woods.

"We shouldn't have ventured to places we are not familiar with," the mother grumbled in a trembling voice. "And whose idea was it?" She stared at her mate, her eyes filling with tears.

"Don't be scared, mother," her son comforted her. "The hunters are after the pheasants. Crows are no good to them."

"We're not safe here," she went on. "The foliage of this tree isn't dense enough to offer us protection."

"Maybe the other side of the woods is quieter. I'm going to find out," her son whispered.

"Don't!" His mother let out a muffled cry. "It's become too dangerous."

"I won't be long, mother. Father will be at your side," said the young crow and was gone.

The shooting eased off for some brief minutes while a different noise, loud and agitating started coming closer.

"What now... What can this rattle mean?" uttered the mother.

"It's the pheasant hunt beaters, I believe that's what they are called," the father said. "The rattle they create is to startle the unfortunate pheasants out of the trees and into the open air to face their fate." He turned and looked at her. She was trembling. He stretched his left wing over her, gave her a soft peck and squeezed her closer.

"We'll be safe my dear, as long as we keep still," he whispered softly.

The shooting was now growing fiercer and fiercer. The two crows sat tight, close to each other, and watched with dread as pheasants were dropping on the ground in twos and in threes, silent, resigned to their fate. They peered down and cringed. The colourful bodies of pheasants littered the forest floor, the terror of death still in their eyes. Two dogs were on the spot carrying the pheasants to their masters. One of them looked up and saw the two crows. He dropped the pheasant and snarled at them, showing his sharp teeth and dribbling disgusting saliva. The mother jumped.

"I can't endure any more of this," she said, choking. "These merciless humans will shoot at anything. We must find our son. I'm off! Follow me!"

The father tried to beat his wings hard to gain height but horror had numbed his wing muscles.

"Wait for me! Wait for me!" He panted. Then he heard the shots.

"Stop firing!" he cried, "I'm only a crow!"

His cry rasped to a squeak and died in his throat. He felt a dull thud, then pain, excruciating pain. Then he plunged into darkness. His body spiralled through the trees and landed on the bluebells.

The young crow saw his mother flying towards him. He heard the shooting getting closer. "Faster! Faster! Try faster, please mother," he cried out.

In the next instant a succession of deafening shots shook the woods. A fair few pheasants plummeted to the ground. There were no more to kill but the frenzied hunters kept on shooting at the empty air, just for fun. But the air wasn't quite empty. The young crow's mother was desperately flying towards her son's cries. A shot rang out. She could feel it close, too close. She let out a husky moan of pain and shut her eyes. Black feathers drifted in the breeze. The young crow saw them.

"Caark, caark, caaaaaark," he started wailing and desperately rising and dipping and clattering through the trees. Then he stopped.

Plato jolted awake. He stood up and looked around him, but saw nothing. He flexed his numbed talons and flew to the ground.

A crow covered in blood lay on the bluebells. Plato choked. He then spotted the wailing crow gliding frantically in circles above the trees before disappearing into the thick ferns.

Plato didn't move. It was when he heard the stirring of dry pine needles behind him that he turned round. He saw the crow drag the black body of a bird and lay it softly on the bluebells. Plato stared at the two bodies all grave and silent.

"This is my mother," the crow uttered with loud whimpers. "The hunters killed my father first. I had to find her." Then he let himself to his grief completely. Tears streamed down his face and choking sobs shook his whole body.

"They are dead," Plato said plainly. "It's unfortunate and dreadful. I am very sorry for you, Crow. This happens in the woods often. Humans get blinded by the thrill of the hunt. Ease your mind, Crow, for there's nothing you can do now."

"I can't leave them like this for the foxes to make a meal of them," wept the crow.

"Would you like to see them…?"

Plato didn't finish what he was about to say but the crow guessed and he nodded.

Plato dug the soft soil under the bluebells, placed the two bodies side by side and covered them. "The bluebells will keep them safe and the foliage of this young fir tree" – he looked up- "will keep the rain and snow away. You can come whenever you feel the need to talk to them."

Then Plato looked him carefully over to make sure the crow had no serious injuries. "There's nothing wrong with you," he said, no cuts, no deep scratches only a few grazes on your wings that will go in no time and won't stop you from flying. Give yourself a few minutes to recover from the shock. I'll stay with you if you want me to. But whatever you decide to do, stay clear of the maddening hunters and you're sure to fly home safely."

"Fly home you said, Owl?" sobbed the crow. "I don't want to go home without them. I'll be terribly alone." He lifted the tip of his wing to wipe a tear but more came rolling down.

"Stop crying," the owl said sternly. "It grieves me to see a bird cry."

"Don't you ever cry, Owl?" wheezed the crow.

"Owls accept things as they come to them. They don't cry, they think," he answered, stroking his brow with the tip of his right wing. Then he looked at the crow and his glassy eyes glinted with sympathy and love for the unfortunate creature.

"I've come up with something that will help you cope with the loss of your parents," he said. "I'll send you to a place where you'll find a new home and make new friends. I've lived round these parts for many long years and most creatures, flying ones, hopping or crawling, know me and they all call me Plato. What name do they call you, Crow?"

"I don't have a name," he answered meekly. "My father called me son and so did my mother. Everyone else called me crow."

"Well then," Plato said cheerfully, "it's time you had one and I think George is a good name for a nice bird such as yourself. What do you say?"

The crow said nothing, but Plato saw a tiny glimmer in his sad eyes and went on.

"Now I want you to calm down and listen. Head towards Sunrise Hill. There's light still left in the sky. When you reach the peak, stop. Far off to your left is the edge of Penny Wood. Look down to your right. Towering cedar, elm and other trees follow the hill down to the valley, then curve and come up again to form a circle. Along with the trees runs the ivy that over the years has knitted an unbroken tangle tying the trees into a solid circular wall. From way back, this glossy green wall has secluded the valley from the outside world. Within that circular wall is Blossom Valley. Families of all kinds of creatures, small, tiny and big, live together as one big family. The head of this family is Thelma, a shrewd spider, but also kind and caring. Bond, the red squirrel and his team guard the ivy wall to keep undesirable visitors away. I'll send a message with Swift, a dear friend of mine. Every spring when his flock fly from the faraway land of Africa, he offers to do messaging and sometimes scouting tasks for me.

"I've never seen a swift nor heard the name until now," said the crow.

"I must tell you then," said Plato with a happy twinkle in his eyes. "Swifts are superb flyers. They rarely come to land, spend almost all their lives in air, even feeding and sleeping in flight. And just in case you bump into one, swifts are black – brown all over, long narrow wings and deeply forked tail. Now make haste before the daylight fades. I know you'll be happy in Blossom Valley and I'll be seeing you quite a lot. Off you go."

The crow, and from now on George the crow, thanked Plato and slipped into the air.

Back on his tree top, the owl watched the sky, certain he would catch sight of George flapping away along the path to Sunrise Hill. But the path remained empty.

There was sadness in Plato's voice when he spoke to himself. "George must have changed his mind. Emotion has taken him back to his home and fellow crows. Pity!"

Two

George changed course in mid-air and followed the path to Crow Lake. He ought to tell his fellow crows who, together with his family, had lived for many years in the copse a short distance from the lake. Plato would understand, he thought.

He wasn't looking forward to this. Crows would gather round him to hear how his parents had died. Some would burst into mourning carks, others would pray that nothing like that ever happened to them. He didn't want to be pitied, treated like an orphan. His parents wouldn't have wanted it. The questions about how his parents had died would never end. The horrific images of his parents' blood-stained bodies would stay alive, and his mind would never ease. He needed a complete change; the wise owl was right. He flapped his wings hard, rose into the clouds and, following Plato's directions, sped towards Sunrise Hill.

At the peak he stopped and took his breath. Penny Wood, was darkening in the distance, its trees massed close together waiting for the night.

Far off to his right he saw the trees. He couldn't see the ivy around them, for the daylight had dimmed and his eyes had grown weary. But the trees were there, looming in the distance, their tops scraping the sky.

All at once, a feeling of uncertainty crept in his mind and troubled him. *Should I have gone to Crow Lake? Shall I carry on for Blossom Valley? Am I making the right decision?*

He looked across to the trees and saw their tops nod in the breeze.

"It's an omen," he said to himself, "the trees are beckoning to me." He let out a deep sigh and took off.

As he neared the ivy wall, he slowed his beat and hovered over. A stout red squirrel sat upright, his tail fluffed up behind him, his head darting in George's direction.

George landed close to him with a brisk sweep of his right wing, and lowered his head in a courteous greeting.

The squirrel jerked his head and stared at him with a sort of curiosity.

"You must be George," he said. "I'm Bond, the head of the guards and these – he pointed to a line of squirrels in shiny red pelts – are my crew."

George greeted them and they in turn gave him tiny smiles then whisked away inside the ivy.

"There're more of us," Bond went on, "guarding the south, north and eastern walls. You'll get the chance to meet them some other time. Swift has already been with Plato's message. I'm pleased to see you, George. Only you took a long time and you got me a little anxious. You're the second newcomer. A while back, we had a ladybird and her three daughters. The mother, Rosa, and her eldest daughter – I don't remember her name – were rude and snappy to my crew." He lowered his voice to a whisper. "I didn't like the sight of them two. They had malice written all over them. I hope they don't cause worse problems than they already have. Now, George, when the gate opens walk through the passage and on to the path. I'd prefer if you didn't fly. Just take the winding path, it'll bring you down to the pond. You can't miss it. Thelma will be meeting you there, and George, come over whenever you feel like a chat. Midday is a good time. We break for lunch. You look puzzled, George, so let me explain. We all work here and take our work seriously. We guard all sides of the wall; other creatures attend to the gardens; still others do their bit to keep Blossom Valley spick and span at all times."

A small gate creaked open and George trotted through a narrow passage and onto the path. There he stopped and blinked in awe.

The great trees, together with the ivy, ran downhill as far as the eye could see before they disappeared round a curve. Alongside the wall, graceful shrubs and bushes pushed the glossy ivy back as if to say, 'we're here too! Give us some space to show off our spring blossoms.'

The tall grass was coloured with forest daisies and flaming red poppies that dipped and rose in the breeze. Mounds and slopes smothered in purple heather and sown with anemones, violets and brilliant yellow buttercups, rolled down to the banks of a stream that flowed peacefully under a dainty bridge then ran off downhill. Everywhere he looked, blossoms burst out on trees, plants and bushes, their delicate scent floating in the air. The beauty was endless. So much more to see, but he shouldn't keep Thelma waiting.

Half way down the hill, a board swinging from an overhanging branch caught his eye. There were arrows with writing on them giving directions to The Ant Village, The Schools. The Music Hall and The Hospital. He couldn't see much of any of them, apart from the hospital that stood on the hill straight ahead. There was a red cross on its wide entrance and on the forecourt rested an ambulance cart. The green writing on its side read, 'For Accidents and Emergencies call Nurse Tawny Owl straight away.'

"Amazing, everything is so amazing," George mumbled. "This place full of such beauty and wonder can't be ordinary. Has the old owl sent me to a… wonderland?"

A pleasant feeling went through him.

"It already feels like home," he mumbled to himself and hurried downhill.

Three

A frog was singing on a lily pad but stopped when he saw the crow and took a huge leap on to the grass. "You must be George," he croaked. "I'm Conti, a humble but talented frog." He puffed himself out. "I'm a tenor frog. I sing classic tunes. I'm happy to see you, George. We heard you were coming but why did you take so long?"

George didn't answer for he hadn't heard. His jaw had dropped open and his eyes widened at the sight of the grandest, most beautiful creatures in shimmering yellows, oranges and blues, fluttering over the pond.

"Are they fair…?"

"They are butterflies," a voice said. He turned round and held his breath. An enormous spider was standing beside him. She had a pleasant appearance that carried superiority and leadership, but also some sadness deep down.

"I am Thelma," the spider said with a wide smile. "Welcome, to Blossom Valley, George. You've come at a good time. We'll be celebrating the arrival of spring soon, as we do every year. We're waiting for the cuckoo to fly over and officially announce it. The butterflies you are marvelling at lived here before any other creature, and so did their ancestors."

George watched them as they gracefully glided over the water lilies and beamed at him.

"Hello, George." They smiled and their eyes shone like diamonds.

"Hello, to you too," he replied in the softest voice he could muster.

"I never knew such creatures existed," George whispered. "So noble and grand."

"They have a long history of grandness," Thelma said. "They are descendants of a kingdom that once stood right here in Blossom Valley. An evil force fell upon it and destroyed it. These few are all there are left of it. The young butterfly in blue is Prince Orpheo and next to him is Princess Estella, his bride to be. The other young ladies are members of the family. In time you will know their names. Sadly, the queen, Estella's mother, hasn't been with us for some long years now. Estella's father, King Iolas, is away on a long journey, but he'll be back to bless his daughter's wedding which is planned for after our Spring Celebration."

George hesitated for a moment then he asked, "What was the evil force?"

The crow's, question startled Thelma and her brow furrowed with annoyance. A newcomer shouldn't be asking questions, she thought to herself, and she wasn't prepared to tell him. Aside from her, only Plato and the butterflies knew, but they never talked about it for the memory was too horrific.

After the kingdom was lost, Blossom Valley plunged into desolate and dark times until all kinds of creatures from neighbouring and far away woods, hills and plains moved in. They built homes and made families and as the years passed Blossom Valley became a large community of all sorts of creatures. They wondered that the rare beauty of the butterflies wasn't that of the ordinary butterflies they had seen fluttering over flowers, in woods and meadows. They made up their minds that these were magical creatures from some distant world and left it at that. They fawned on them but otherwise regarded them as members of the community like everyone else.

George was bewitched by them and it was normal that he'd be curious and, Thelma considered, George did no wrong in wanting to know more about the lost kingdom. After all, he wouldn't have asked if she hadn't mentioned it. She shouldn't have frowned at a creature who had been orphaned only hours ago and prayed that George hadn't noticed her annoyance.

It took her a while before the words came out of her mouth.

"The story goes back many years, George, and it's best left alone. You'll soon get to know everyone here including the butterflies who spend the mornings at the schools. They teach the ant classes, music and singing."

George looked baffled and Thelma noticed it. "Our ant choir is one of the best in the ant world. The bigger creatures, those who want to learn music or dancing, go to the Music Hall. Our butterflies who are gifted with exceptional voices teach them singing and Mr B Rabbit, a tap-dancing champion, teaches them to tap-dance. Our community is made up of families of all kinds and sizes of creatures. Each family lives its own private life, and all have a say in our community. All families we join together in one peaceful greater family. We gather at dusk to mix together, hear one another's news or stories and have fun. What we do not allow in our community"- her voice rose – "is bullying or harming one another, and of course we unite against any threat to our community."

Her voice was clear and determined and George thought that a spider, even one her size couldn't lead such a large community unless she had some secret or perhaps magical power hidden inside her.

"Goodness!" Thelma shouted and George jolted out of his thoughts. "I've got carried away. I'm sorry if I've bored you, George. Don't look so apprehensive. Cheer up. We're glad to have you in our family. You'll be happy with us."

A loud caw made George jump.

"It's the crow family," Thelma explained. "They are on the ivy wall, waiting to meet you. We'll see you later, George. Your friends will bring you down to the gathering."

Four

A pale moon was floating over Blossom Valley when George and his fellow crows came down to the gathering.

"Some of us flock up on the elm tree," said Alphie, one of the younger crows. "You'll find others by the white rock where Speedo the snail tells them stories. And if you hear screams and cheers, it'll be the crows and rabbits kicking the conker, on a stretch of trimmed grass we call the Football Clearing. You'll find it by the cluster of chestnut trees. Have a wander around, George. There's a lot to see."

"I'll do just that. Thanks, Alphie," said George and trotted off.

Squabbling loudly, the blackbirds flocked up onto the elm tree and kept on bickering among themselves until the wrens flew in. Their sweet evening trills drifted across the valley and all the creatures fell silent, enjoying the tranquillity of the dusk. Only Robin Redbreast wouldn't stop fidgeting. He kept chirping and frolicking from bush to bush.

"Can't you stay still for five minutes, Robin? You're giving me a headache watching you," a pot-bellied sparrow complained in a shrilly chirp. "Relax, like all of us are trying to do."

Robin drew his feathers tight round him in anger. "Of all birds, to have been insulted by a common sparrow," he mumbled, but loud enough to be heard. Then he flew away.

Red squirrels and hedgehogs were spread out upon a mossy bank, the squirrels chattering away and munching at the same time, their jaws moving up and down with machine-like precision.

"We can't understand a word you're saying," an old hedgehog grumbled. "Empty your mouth before you talk. No manners!"

"Granny Hedgehog…" A squirrel tried to say something, but Granny Hedgehog, huffing loudly through her nose, was waddling away. She settled with a group of rabbits and watched the tap-dancing rabbits practising for the upcoming tap-dancing competition.

Loud voices and screams were coming from the chestnut trees and George hurried towards them, eager to see how crows could ever manage to play football. He opened his mouth in amazement when he saw them running between the rabbits' legs, trying to steal the conker and keep it away from their half. The conker suddenly landed on the foot of the black rabbit who gave it an almighty kick and sent it flying towards the crows' goal post. The crow goal keeper jumped up, stretched out his wings and hit the conker with such force, it raced back and straight into the rabbits' net.

The crows clapped with their wings, danced, screamed and cheered and George joined them in their excitement.

"I wish you could teach me a few tricks. I'd love to learn the game," George told the crow goal keeper.

"We'll be glad to," he said. "Join us at the training tomorrow or any early afternoon of the week. Call me Ted and you are George. Pleased, to meet you," said the goal keeper, wiping the sweat that was running down his nose.

On his way down to the pond George stumbled by the white rock and paused to watch the snail who sat on the rock, his feelers bobbing up and down and his tiny eyes sparkling. Just below the rock, on a small patch of soft ground, hedgehogs, squirrels and ants, crows and sparrows were spread, all still and silent, listening, their eyes widening here, narrowing there, then bursting into laughter.

"That's all until tomorrow," said the snail. "It's time we went down to the pond."

* * *

"We're in for some real excitement," the frog croaked excitedly and everyone's head turned towards the tall fir tree where Bond, the red squirrel, was tying a vine between two branches at the very top.

"What's that?" asked George.

"It's a tightrope," Conti the frog explained. "Bond and his team will perform acrobatics on it."

The creatures burst out into wild whistling when Bond stepped on the tightrope, swinging his head and body to a rhythm. He bowed and, flipping a series of backward somersaults, reached the end of the rope and disappeared into the tree. Within seconds he was back on the vine, spinning round and round in a succession of cartwheels, slowly at first, then a little faster, and then with such speed that he became a blurred ball of red fluff.

The spectators erupted into delirious screaming, clapping and stamping, but in the next instant everyone hushed and held their breath. The knots on one end of the vine came undone and Bond was heading for a nasty crash on the rocks that lay on the ground right beneath him. The creatures sprang to their feet, oohing and aahing, for the red squirrel was but a couple of inches away from crashing onto the sharp edges of the jagged rocks. But at the last instant the frayed end of the vine swayed in front of his face. Bond snatched it with his teeth, swung wildly in the air and landed on the ground. He saw Thelma standing close by and Tawny Owl, the nurse, next to her.

"Sorry, if I worried everyone," he said, then bowed.

In the midst of all the excitement, Conti plunged into his pond, surfaced with a series of spluttering gasps and started his tune. The more excited he got, the louder he sang. Some creatures clapped their wings over their ears.

"Give us some peace, you noisy green beast!" the blackbirds moaned. "It's been a hard day."

The frog stopped and leapt close to George. "The other creatures don't seem to mind my singing," he sputtered. "It's them, the blackbirds, always whinging and fussing. It's in their nature, I'm telling you."

"I'm sure they didn't mean your singing isn't good," said George, feeling sorry for the frog. "It's possible they've had a hard day, for the sky can be a dangerous place. Predators perhaps, and have you thought that classical tunes may not be everybody's taste, especially at this hour?"

Conti's wet eyes, full of sincerity, stared at George.

"I knew you were a kindly and understanding creature the minute I saw you, George," he said. Then he stretched his neck close to George's ear. "Weird things are happening and I need to talk to you about them. I tell Thelma. She won't listen but I know you will. There're these scary groans and muffled cries I hear in my pond when the moon becomes full, and…"

At that moment Thelma walked across the grass. She raised her hands and spoke. "Good evening everyone."

"Good evening," said the voices from across the valley.

"Firstly, I would like all of us to say a welcoming hello to George, the crow, who joined our family today."

"Hello, George!" everyone shouted.

"Hello, to you all," George answered.

Then Thelma clapped her hands. "Are all the members of our families here?"

"Yes," came the reply.

"Are there any problems to be discussed?"

"No," the creatures chorused.

"Then, let us all sing our *Good Night Song*."

Every creature threw their heads back and sang.

> *Our day is about to end*
> *Soon night will descend but only for a short while*
> *Our pale moon will now ride in the sky*
> *To put on her silver dress for the night*
>   *and switch on the stars*
> *That will twinkle over our valley*
>   *until the night will glide*
> *Into a dawn joyful and bright*
> *Good night everyone. Sleep tight.*

The creatures made their way home while George trotted over to Thelma. He was surprised to see Plato talking to her.

"Hello, George," said Plato. I can tell you're settling in and I'm pleased for you."

"I am," said George. "How can I ever repay you, Plato?"

"Just be my friend," he replied, then took to the sky, heading for Penny Wood and his night hunt.

Five

George felt tired and couldn't wait to get to his roost. He was about to get off the ground when the branches of a bush swung across his path and a fearsome ladybird darted out.

"Oh!" George gasped.

"What's the matter, Crow?" the ladybird screeched. "You haven't seen a ladybird before?"

"Forgive me, lady," George replied with a polite bow. "I'm the new crow, George."

"I know who you are," she snapped. "No news escapes me, and I'm Rosa, if you care to know."

"I didn't see any ladybirds at the gathering," George said hesitantly.

"You didn't cause we don't go there."

"Why?"

"Cause they don't like us and we don't like them. They've looked down on me and my daughters ever since we came. They've got eyes only for them… the butterflies and we hate them for that. What have they got over us, I ask you, Crow? We are five spot ladybirds, the rarest of the species. Take a look at my shell, Crow," she said and swivelled round. In the remains of the sunset glow that slanted through the trees, her shell shone a brilliant red tinged with orange, and her spots glistened like five black gems.

"You see, Crow," she beamed with pride. "We're special, we're not common. She, the spider, calls Estella, Princess, and Orpheo, Prince." She curled her lips into a sneer.

"Rubbish! Where there's a prince or a princess, there's a palace. Am I right, Crow? Go on correct me if you think I'm wrong. Now I'm asking you, Crow, did you see a palace in Blossom Valley?"

"No I didn't," he stammered. "This is my first day here. I couldn't see everything."

"No you didn't, and you never will, crow, cause there isn't one."

George's mind drifted back to what Thelma had said. 'Their Kingdom was destroyed.'

"I know what you're thinking, Crow, cause I heard all that the spider told you. If ever there was a palace, it can't have disappeared in a huff of smoke. There would be some remains scattered or buried somewhere in this place. I've looked and found nothing. I'm telling you, Crow, it's her, the spider, has made up the myth that her and her butterflies live by.

She gets stroppy every time my daughters go near them, accusing them of bullying her butterflies. She claimed my Heather tried to drown prince Orpheo. That was a lie the old wrinkly frog made up and she believed him. Why are they so precious to her? I'm asking you, Crow. And who is she, a spider, even her size, to be the head of this vast place? It's odd, isn't it? Something weird, spooky, goes on in here, I'm telling you, Crow. She wants to see the back of us. I know. I'm not daft. We'll go, but not before…"

"Rosa," George interrupted, "it saddens me to hear a beautiful ladybird such as you, use harsh words and bear awful thoughts against fellow creatures. They're all a big family here who respect and look out for one another. You have stayed apart. Try and find the reason why. Is it jealousy? Is it hatred? Then get rid of it. Join the family and you and your daughters will feel a lot happier, trust me."

Rosa stared at George, listening to every word he spoke in utter stillness. Maybe, she thought, the crow was right. Change, get rid of her jealousy be a better creature, be family with the spider and the butterflies. Be nice to them? No.! She jerked as if she were waking from a nightmare. *No, I was born like this and no one told me there was another way. Why change now? I enjoy it as I am. I won't change. Not now that me and my Heather are working on a wicked plan that will shudder the spider and the whole Valley for many years to come.* She thrust her sneering face close to George's.

"Well, I'll be blowed!" she screeched. "Trust a stupid crow to come up with a speech as stupid as this. Join the family! Ha!" She gave George a black glare and took off in a huff.

George stayed rooted to the ground, too upset to move. All sorts of thoughts and questions whirled inside his head but all he needed now was his roost to lie in.

His fellow crows were nestled, all snug and fast asleep. He tried to push all thoughts out of his head, but as darkness gathered round him he felt lonely. He thought of his parents and broke into silent sobs. The crows stirred.

"Hey," whispered, Alphie, from the next roost. "Don't cry. You miss your parents, we understand, but you're not alone now. We're here for you, all of us. Try and get some sleep. Things will look brighter in the morning, you'll see."

Alphie's kind words brought more tears to his eyes. He felt bad for disturbing them, so he quietly slipped out of his roost. He found a thick bush, hunched his head deep inside his wings and closed his eyes.

Six

A pink dawn was breaking when George opened his bleary eyes the next day. He took a gulp of fresh air and flapped his wings to exercise their muscles. He spent time preening his feathers and then set off for the pond.

He'd walked just a few paces when he heard light pattering behind him. He feared the ladybird might be following him and spun round.

"Good morning, Thelma," he said, relief written all over his face. "I'm glad I'll have the chance to talk to you, if you're not too busy."

"I'm never too busy to listen, George, anything wrong? You look apprehensive."

George hesitated.

"Well?" Thelma prompted, her eyes widening with curiosity.

"Rosa, the ladybird, bumped into me after the gathering. She knew my name before I…"

"Rosa misses very little," Thelma interrupted, "for she spends a lot of her time watching and earwigging. What did she have to say, anyway?" she asked, trying to sound unconcerned.

George couldn't bring himself to repeat Rosa's hateful words and thoughts. "Not much," he replied, "but her tongue was unkind when she spoke about you and the butterflies."

Thelma let out a long deep sigh then rested her eyes upon George. "We welcomed Rosa and her daughters a while back. The sob-story she told us touched us all in our community. I

23

now wonder if there was any truth in it. They kept themselves to themselves for a time and we respected that. But as time passed they became jealous of the butterflies for their beauty and the voices they're gifted with. Amongst other things, Heather, Rosa's eldest daughter, took a fancy to Prince Orpheo and kept shadowing him. When she was told to stay away, she turned vengeful. With her sisters' help, she tried to drown Prince Orpheo in the pond. Had Conti not been there, the prince would be dead today. Then they turned against the butterflies, especially Estella. They kept teasing and bullying them in a spiteful manner. I reprimanded them severely, of course I did. It is my job to protect the weak and vulnerable, especially the butterflies who are precious to me and Blossom Valley."

While Thelma was talking, all sorts of thoughts tumbled inside George's head. "Why are the butterflies so precious to her? Is she their mother, turned into a spider by the evil force? Did she commit some dreadful deed and was punished or…? Phew! Too many riddles for my brain to guess," he muttered silently to himself. "I won't trouble my brain again. The riddle or riddles will be answered one day. I'll just have to wait."

Suddenly, swirls of beautiful music drifted across the valley, followed by heavenly singing.

"They've started!" Thelma said with a little jump. "It's the last rehearsal before our celebration. Why don't you come along with me, George?"

"I will," George answered, "after I've said hello to Conti and asked him to join me."

***

All morning, Conti had been preparing the story of his life. He went over it time and again to make sure his brain had taken it all in, and would keep it there until George came round. He was so happy that he capered off across the grass, whirling and hopping and croaking until he bumped into George.

"What are you up to, Conti?" George asked.

"I'm happy, that's all. I hope you'll spare a little time with me to hear my life story," said Conti. "I've got it ready up here." He touched his head.

"I wouldn't miss it for the world, but after we've been to the Music Hall to listen to the rehearsals. We're both invited."

"We?" Conti asked, panting.

"Yes, and they've already started. Can you not hear the music?"

A host of small birds had lined the tree branches by the Music Hall and were listening to the music, some quietly repeating the flute trills.

"Look who's here, the sparrow," Robin Redbreast, chirped. "You know that only song birds are gifted with the chords to trill. Sparrows aren't. So why are you here?"

The sparrow put his head down and flew away.

"You've gone too far, this time Robin," a wren scolded him.

"He was harsh on me at the gathering," Robin protested.

"He didn't criticize your voice. It was your frolicking which can be annoying at times. I believe an apology wouldn't go amiss. You called him common and that's cruel."

"You're right, wren," Robin admitted. "I'll do it straight away."

The music that flowed from the flute was heavenly and the voices so magical, so pure and beautiful that it brought tears to George's eyes.

Conti was enchanted. It showed on his face. His mouth fell open and his eyes were glued to the flute Prince Orpheo was playing.

"Call me crazy," Conti whispered in George's ear, "but that flute isn't ordinary. It's magical. It's playing on its own. It takes Orpheo's breath and plays by itself. Didn't you notice?"

George shook his head.

"He barely touched the stops. You know what I'm talking about?"

George shook his head.

"Stops are the holes in all wind instruments. You blow through the flute and your fingers have to go over the stops to form the notes. My tenor explained it to me. I'll tell you all about him later. I'm now going to leave quietly. Come when you're ready."

**

Conti was making loud gargling noises as if trying to get rid of something stuck in his throat. George thought the old frog was choking. Only when he got closer did he realise that Conti was preparing to sing. His chest was stretched out, his head thrown back and his eyes closed. He opened his mouth and let the first notes flow out slow and soft, almost whispering, gradually getting louder. George had never seen a frog with such a gleeful expression on his face, nor heard a frog sing like this. As the song reached its crescendo, Conti flung his arms up in the air. His mouth opened wide and his tongue danced inside it. Then two tears rolled down his face.

"Bravo!" George exclaimed and clapped his wings hard.

"I've never put such effort into my singing before. I did it for you, my friend," Conti panted, his eyes gleaming orange and green in the morning sun. "I hope you liked it."

"I did, my friend," said George. "It was brilliant, but why the tears?"

"They are tears of joy, George. The days are long with nothing much to do. I have no mates like most of you creatures and I get lonely, I do. My years are piling up. Singing keeps me going. You know how I came to sing classic tunes?" he asked and immediately set about answering his question.

"Years back I lived in the pond of a grand house. A famous tenor had rented it and a fine human he was. He named me Conti, after an Italian tenor. He was Italian himself. I was allowed to hop inside the house and watch him sing. He'd practised for hours before he left for the Opera House. Then I'd hop into my pond where I would go over the tunes I had heard.

Sadly, the tenor moved away and I lost a good friend. New people bought the house. They filled the pond, and I was lucky I wasn't buried under the gravel. After that, I wandered for days on end looking for water. A severe drought that year had dried ponds, creeks and dykes. I carried on, dragging my legs behind me under the scorching sun until I collapsed on the parched grass. A bird must have spotted me from high above. I knew it was an owl, for I vaguely heard his hoot in the distant sky. He came down and spoke to me. My eyelids were stuck tight and my limbs almost dead, and guess what? The owl was telling me of a place where there was water and giving me directions to get there. I forced one eyelid open, just a crack and saw him.

"Let me be, Owl," I muttered with the little breath that was left in me. "Can't you see I'm dying?"

"Plato is my name," he snapped, "and no, I can't see you're dying, for I won't let you." He grabbed me by my back legs and brought me to this pond. I've been happy here, I have, and everyone has been good to me. Only, if it weren't for these terrible things that are happening in my pond."

"What's happening in your pond, Conti?" George asked, looking worried.

"It wasn't this bad in the beginning and with my hearing not being so good, I could barely hear them. It has got worse, much louder, in recent times. When the moon becomes full muffled groans and cries of pain and anger come from deep below the water. Then there's the eerie shrills of the bats that flitter over the water lilies. Sometimes they come skimming over my head and they scare me out of my skin, they do."

"Bats are blind and can't see you. That's why they bump into you. There's nothing nasty about the bats. For all you know they come over for a sip of water."

"Bats are witches," the frog said, "didn't you know? Well, I'm telling you, bats are witches and come over to communicate with whatever magic, witches and stuff are buried deep in the pond."

"You're talking nonsense now."

"I'm talking about magic, my friend. There's a lot of magic in this world of ours, didn't you know? Well, I'm telling you, there's magic in the air, the woods, mountains and valleys, in lakes and ponds. You can't see it cause it's invisible and secret. Only sometimes you can feel it and sometimes hear it. I've heard stories that would make the skin at the back of your neck tingle."

"You don't believe in old tales, do you, Conti?"

"I do believe the stories or tales as you call them, my friend," the frog replied stubbornly.

"From way back in time, witches cast spells on humans turning them into mice, princesses into spiders and princes into…" His eyes rolled round and round, gleaming with excitement and his mouth curved into a smile. "Princes into frogs…" he muttered his mouth moving up and down as if he were silently talking to somebody. Then all of a sudden he started to shake his head violently left and right, up and down like a demented frog.

"What's the matter, Conti?" George asked worriedly.

"I've been trying to ask my brain questions and the matter is, it can't take them in cause it's full of other stuff, mainly my life story, and now that you've heard it, it can go. I need to shake it empty so it can take my questions and hopefully give me some answers."

He gave a sudden jerk and as his head dropped over the still water, his reflection, green and remote, glared back at him. Conti went rigid and silent like a frog out of a mould.

Seconds later, he looked at George, the skin round his wet eyes creased into rings of sad wrinkles. "Nah…" He sighed. "All my brain is doing, is showing me images of a frog, a wrinkly old frog. Me. I reckon what it is trying to tell me, is that I've always been a plain frog and not one with a crown on his head."

"Whew!" George puffed. "You had me worried, my friend, and I'm glad you've sorted it out. As for me, I know I've always been a crow and right now I'm off to Penny Wood."

"What are you going to Penny Wood for, George?"

But George was already soaring across the sky.

***

Penny Wood was silent that morning. Only the light stirring of the treetops could be heard and a woodpecker's faint hammering at some distant tree.

Anxiety crept inside George as he circled low over the trees looking for the bluebells. It was some time before he spotted them. His heart pounding in his chest, he came down.

"No!" he gasped. The bluebells lay trodden on one side and there was a footprint on the ground close by. George sat staring in dismay.

He suddenly straightened up. "Hold on," he said loudly to himself, "the soil hasn't been disturbed and this is not a fox's paw. It's a human's, a hunter's boot." He looked around. The bluebells where he'd left his parents were under a fir tree and the ferns were nearby.

"This is the wrong part of the woods," he uttered. He breathed a sigh of relief and flew over to the other side.

Penny Wood was at its thickest there, and the haze that still lingered over the tree tops blotted his vision. He flew just above the trees, round and round, in a straight line, then across and always ended up where he'd started. Frustration and despair got the better of him and he broke out in loud carks.

Suddenly, a blinding fork of lightning tore the sky apart and at once the thunder crashed somewhere close by. Black clouds darkened the sky and the trees stood still and silent waiting for the storm. George took shelter in the foliage of a tree, crossed his wings around him and waited for the rain to pour down.

Time passed and neither storm nor even a drop of rain appeared. George looked up. The sun was pushing the black clouds back. The darkness gradually thinned and a bright light spilled out on to the forest floor.

It was then that George realised the tree he'd sheltered in was the young fir tree. Relief and joy overtook him. He now knew exactly where his parents lay.

Tendrils of forest creepers had found their way to the bluebells and had snagged on them. George pushed them to the side, parted the bluebells and saw the tip of a black feather.

"I've found you," he sighed. "I want you to know that I'm missing you terribly. I've found a new home and I'll be happy there. I haven't been to Crow Lake to see the relatives yet, but…"

"Oi, you're talking to yourself!" A bird's sing-song voice cut him short. "That's the first sign of madness, so my grandfather reckons," the bird went on and flew down beside him. "You're a crow, yeah right?"

"And you are an arrogant and rude jackdaw," George replied reproachfully. "Where did you learn this silly language?"

"I picked it up from young humans who stick around our area. It's cool, isn't it? I only use it when I'm away from my parents, if I ever am. That's why I left. They want to keep me under their guard. They reckon they know best," he added scornfully.

"Never scorn your parents' anxiety, young fellow," George scolded him. "They care about your safety and yes, parents know best."

"We live in rocks," said the jackdaw. "I want to see some of the rest of the world – woods, rivers and valleys – and I want to do it by myself."

"Fine, you've done that. Now it's time you went home. The woods are quiet today but there're all sorts of dangers in the sky. I mean predators. So be vigilant."

George straightened the bluebells and placed the creepers over them. He closed his eyes and remained silent as if in prayer.

"I'll be back soon," he whispered and took off.

Seven

Crow Lake was quite a flight away but George had made his mind up it was time to tell his fellow crows about his parents and his new life in Blossom Valley. He was some few beats away when he halted in mid-air. A huge mushroom of black smoke hung over the lake and beyond, tongues of fierce red fire leapt through the trees of the copse. Crows flew frantically around, passing on cries of danger and alarm.

The warning seemed to have come too late, for through his stinging eyes George saw screaming crows, a wing or tail on fire, plunging into the lake then floating lifeless on the still water. On the far left side of the copse the fire wasn't at his fiercest yet but the wind was changing and would soon fan it on.

George's throat was dry and his eyes stung. He brought one of his wings over his mouth to filter the smoky air, took long breaths and dived down.

Choking chicks were squawking wildly in their nests while the mothers, numbed by the horror around them, were doing nothing but wailing.

"Don't sit like stoned crows. Wake up!" he ordered. "Get on the ground, cup your wings and catch the chicks as I'll be dropping them. Take them to the heath. The bracken will keep them cool."

A few burning trees away, a mother had fallen over a nest at the very top, weeping and mourning.

"Mourn for your babies when they're dead, and they'll soon be if you don't pull yourself together." He lifted her by the neck and dropped her on the ground. "Now catch your babies," he yelled at her, "and run to the bracken, fast."

In the meantime, those crows who were still able to help, took the injured to the bracken where the breeze from the lake was cooling the heat of the fire.

"It's all the humans' fault," an old crow said. "Mindless young folk throwing live cigarettes on the forest floor. No respect for nature, no regret for lost life. Don't they listen to their parents and school teachers who tell them that without nature there won't be life? Look at what they've done to us, the misery they've caused."

A desperate cark suddenly cut through the smoky air and made George jump.

"Don't go!" the old crow urged. "It's become too dangerous."

George ignored him and went off.

Far off on the western bank of the lake, all on its own stood a young tree that had been counting its blessings the fire had spared it. But the fire had shown no real mercy. A spark had now travelled in the wind and set it alight.

On the top branch, sat an old crow, motionless but carking his throat out.

George shook him violently. "Move!" he yelled.

The crow stared at him and carried on carking.

George grabbed him by the neck and brought him to safety. "Fly!" he ordered. "Use your wings!"

The crow didn't move. The shock had taken his sight, speech and hearing away. The rescue team pulled him to the bracken.

George skirted the lake over and over to make sure no injured had been left behind. The young tree had burnt completely but it still stood smouldering and smoking, refusing to fall. In the end, it yielded to its fate. Its black skeleton crashed down, exploding red hot sparks everywhere.

A whiff of burning reached George's nostrils. One spark had landed on his chest, scorching his feathers. He felt the heat stinging his flesh and heard it sizzling.

"Aaargh! Aaargh!" he yelped and rushed to the water.

He looked up at the sky. "If only I could see Swift and send a message to Plato," he mumbled, his breathing slowly trailing off into silence.

***

"Why the downcast face on such a beautiful morning, Conti?" Plato asked as he glided down to the pond.

"George wasn't at the gathering," Conti replied broodingly, "and Alfie, his mate, said his roost wasn't slept in last night. He's gone back to Crow Lake, where his home was, and he isn't coming back, I'm telling you. It's my fault. It's what I said. I've scared him."

"What are you talking about, creature?" Plato frowned.

"I told him scary things and stuff."

"What stuff, Conti?" Plato insisted.

Conti broke out in loud sobs. "I don't know. Stop muddling my brain, asking questions one after another too fast. My brain is loaded with my own questions. It can't take any more. It is confused and sad, very sad, cause it's all my fault. That's what my brain is telling me."

At that instant, Alphie flew over.

"I'm glad I found you, Plato," he said, panting. "The copse at Crow Lake has burnt down. Many dead and many injured. Me, and the rest of Blossom Valley crows are heading there to offer help, but it is medical help they need urgently. I thought of Tawny Owl."

"Did you see George? Is he safe, Alphie?" Conti spluttered.

"Can't answer that, Conti, cause I flew straight here," was Alphie's reply.

The frog let out a deafening croak and plunged into his pond.

Shortly afterwards Tawny Owl and Alphie, a straw first-aid box hanging from their beaks, took to the sky. Plato followed.

Tawny Owl was hard at work straight away, running from the chicks to the injured as fast as she could and in utter silence.

"Is George, alive?" Plato asked an old crow, his voice tense with anxiety.

The old crow blinked, trying to see through the smoke. "I don't know about that, Owl," he said. "There's no one called George here. We're all crows. Unless you mean the hero -he was a Crow Lake fellow like us. He saved the chicks. He saved others as well. He's dead now."

Plato's heart lurched heavily inside his chest.

"Heroes die first," the old crow went on in a wheezy voice. "That's what I said to him when they brought him back from the lake. He didn't hear me cause he'd passed out, they told me."

"Passed out?" Plato puffed with relief.

"That's what I said, Owl, dead, passed out it makes no difference. It means the same thing, doesn't it?"

"Plato!" Alphie called from the bracken, "George is lying here seriously injured."

Tawny Owl was beside him in a jiffy.

"See to the others first, Tawny Owl. I can wait," George said, groaning with pain.

"I know my job," Tawny Owl replied firmly. "You've got a nasty burn, red as the heart of a beetroot. The remedy I'm going to apply will sting and burn horribly for some few seconds. So feel free to jump up and down, or scream your head off, until the pain eases off, then rest.

Plato took Tawny Owl aside. He pulled something from deep inside his left wing and ceremoniously handed it to her.

"This," he said in a deep, earnest voice, "is a sacred old remedy. My master, the Great Owl of Delphi, left it with me before he flew back to the mountain of Parnassus in Greece. He said, "When I die Plato, and I shall one day, I want to be in the high mountains and hills that surround Delphi, my homeland. You know of course that we owls originate from Greece. My old master told me that one of his very ancient ancestors sat on the shoulder of Athena, the goddess of Athens, guiding her with his wisdom. This remedy has great powers. So use it wisely and consider it precious."

Tawny Owl looked intrigued and fascinated. "You have never talked about him before, Plato, Why not?"

"Because the opportunity has but now risen, Tawny Owl," he answered plainly.

After Tawny Owl left the bracken, silence fell, as the crows, exhausted by the horror of the fire and relieved of their pain, nodded off.

It was sometime in late afternoon that George, together with a few others, left the bracken and slowly walked to where a number of crows had gathered around the old crow whose spirit much brighter now, was talking about happenings long in the past. Plato was still there. George trotted over to him and spoke.

"I'm grateful, Plato. All of us at Crow Lake are. Without you and Alphie, our Blossom Valley fellow crows but mostly, without Tawny Owl's medical assistance, we wouldn't have coped. I won't be coming back to Blossom Valley, for as you'll appreciate I'm needed here. We have to find a new home, and because it's all farm land around here, we'll have to travel far to find trees."

Plato fell silent, stroking his brow, as he did when he was

going through his thoughts. "I believe I've found a good solution," he said. "Why travel far in search of a new home when Blossom Valley is already a home to a crow family? There are lots of uninhabited trees in Blossom Valley and many herons in Penny Reeds who are brilliant architects of nest building. They're good friends of Blossom Valley and will be happy to help us. We'll transport the chicks, the injured and the frail. Our ambulance cart sits outside the hospital and those creatures who pull it are the fastest and most reliable hares in the region. Talk it over among you and decide. I'll be back tomorrow," he concluded and took off.

"What was he talking about? Is he serious?" a crow with a patch on his left eye asked.

"He's an owl," the old crow blurted out. "Owls never speak words that aren't serious and wise. Remember that."

Eight

For years the herons had built their nests in the reeds along Penny River. Early each spring they'd fly into Blossom Valley to pick up the twigs that the creatures had saved for them. They'd become good friends with everyone and were only too happy to build as many nests as were needed.

Everyone came out and watched with great admiration as the herons, flapping their massive wings in stately slow motion, flew in. They landed on the tall grass, and without much ado started work.

To speed the build and save the herons from flying to and fro from the twig-heap to the trees, it was arranged that the big birds, rabbits, Conti and a few squirrels, would transport the twigs to the bottom of each tree where the squirrels would clamp them with their teeth, race up the trees, hand them to the herons and race down again.

So it was not long before a large number of nests were ready for the crows and their babies to move in. Slowly they got used to their new home, felt secure and happy and life in Blossom Valley went on as before.

**

Then one evening, Speedo the snail wasn't at the gathering.

"Search in the strawberry garden. He often goes there to have a rest or a nap," shouted some ants.

"Take a look in the lettuce patch," said a rabbit.

"No need for any of that," Conti croaked loudly. "He's gone. He left me a message. Sorry it went out of my mind.

My brain refuses to store sad messages. It lets them slip out. Only it's gradually coming to me now. He said he had been feeling lonely, yearning to find his fellow snails. He said he was sorry he didn't announce it at the last gathering, cause he couldn't bring himself to tell his crowd. Besides, they would have tried to talk him out of it. You can't blame him, can you? A creature wants to be with his own kind. That's how nature has made us." Conti burst into loud sobs, took a huge leap and dived into his pond.

Speedo had only crawled a short distance away from Blossom Valley when George found him the next day.

"Conti told us. Your audience are sad you've left them. They miss you we all miss you, Speedo. We are all one family."

"I've felt lonely for a long time, George," sobbed Speedo. "I've been bored of life. I desperately yearn to see my friends, my own kind." Tears gathered in his tiny eyes as he continued.

"I lost my family long ago. They were caught under the tractor's wheels. It wasn't the farmer's fault. He was reversing out of the barn. They shouldn't have been there. But I was left among friends, my own kind. We were a happy bunch.

Sometime back, there was a severe storm. A horrific gust of wind blew through the farm, lifted sheds, uprooted plants and bushes and tossed them long distances away. I was tossed up on the edge of Blossom Valley. I'd been beaten on all sides and I stayed in my shell, waiting to die.

It was Bond, the red squirrel and his team, the kindest of creatures, who brought me back to life. They kept talking to me, urging me to come out, telling me about the beauty of Blossom Valley, the butterflies, the frog. I have been happy in Blossom Valley, I'm not complaining. But I can't help thinking about my fellow snails. I dream of Dyke Farm. I need to know what happened to my friends. It will take me ages. I don't care if it's forever, but one day I shall reach Dyke

Farm. I long, to hear the yew tell her young lambs, stories. That's how I became a storyteller myself. She told them a new story every day. I asked her how come she knew so many different stories. You know what she said? *I make them up as I go along.* So I started doing the same with my family and friends and I was successful."

George had gone quiet, carried into deep thought. Then he spoke. "What would you say if I offered to make your journey shorter than ages, shorter than forever, and get you to Dyke Farm in a few short hours from now?"

"How do you mean?" Speedo huffed, his antenna bobbing and his eyes glistening.

"I will fly you there. Get on my back and hold tight. I'll take it easy. I'll try to make the flight as smooth as possible."

"Are you alright up there, Speedo? You're too quiet," George called some few minutes after the take-off.

"I'm still in my shell, George," Speedo replied in a trembling voice.

"Has it not been safe so far? Don't you trust me, Speedo?" George sounded disappointed.

"Oh, my dear friend, of course I trust you. But from crawling to being in the air is scary and I'm such a coward."

Speedo decided it was time he confronted his fear, and scooted out of his shell. He was glad he did. It was a breathtaking spectacle as he watched fields, meadows and the hedgerows rolling away beneath him.

"George!" he screamed in his tiny little voice, "look down! Yelping hounds, some beautiful horses and their posh riders. Why are they running like a pack of demented wolves?"

"It is the Fox Hunt, Speedo, the privileged humans' game," George explained. "The hounds are following a poor fox's scent, aiming to ambush him somewhere in the undergrowth and I can't even bear to think what the savage hounds will do to him."

"You mean they'll kill him – tear him apart?" Speedo's voice wobbled.

"They will," said George, his voice cracking with emotion. "It is the game of the elite humans. It gives them pleasure to see a creature being killed, blood being spilled. They do it for fun."

"No creature should die just for the sake of fun," Speedo cried, his eyes filling with tears.

"But they do, Speedo. Humans can be very cruel to creatures. They think that we can't feel pain, the loss of a dear parent, or friend. My parents were killed just for the sake of fun. I saw it happen in front of my very eyes." George choked and tears clouded his eyes. He had to come down.

"George, I think we're here. Take a look at that faded writing on the old gate. Does it say *Dyke Farm*? Are we here?"

"We are, Speedo. I hope you find your friends soon."

"You made my dream come true, George, I'll always remember the thrill of flying but most of all your kindness. Leave me here. I'm at home now."

"I'll be back in two days to see how you got on," said George. "Be by the barn so I don't miss you. Good luck, my friend!" he called flapping his wings and rising into the sky.

Two days later George was at the farm. The place was deserted. The roofs of the barns had been blown away, doors and windows were hanging from rusted hinges. There was no sign of any farm animals and no sign of Speedo. He paid several visits to the farm and in the end he gave up.

It was on a wet morning months later that George spotted two snails crawling on the ground and landed close to them.

"I'm very sorry if I stood you up," said Speedo, "but I had wandered too far. This is Sally, the sister of my best friend,

Derek. Most of our fellow snails have vanished, blown to god knows where. I found Sally by chance. She was also searching for them.

"I'm glad for you, Speedo. At least you have Sally now. Would you like a lift to the valley?"

"Thank you, George," said Sally. "You've already done enough. Besides, we'd rather get there by ourselves. There's still so much more to catch up with."

Everyone was happy to see Speedo back on the white rock, this time with Sally by his side. His audience had grown bigger. They were all keen to hear about his flight on George's back, his desperate search for his fellow snails, and how he bumped into Sally.

Nine

And so the days passed, and each dawned as glorious as the one before until one morning, totally unexpectedly, Blossom Valley woke up under a blanket of grey mist. Not a single whisper of wind or breeze stirred and a strange hush had taken hold of the entire valley. Even the sun wouldn't show up, as if it had made up its mind to take the morning off.

But after it had enjoyed a long lie in, its glowing face popped up over the tip of Sunrise Hill and came blazing through the gaps of the trees. It turned the mist into pink haze, silvered the grass, and turned the dew drops into sparkling crystals.

Perched high on the elm tree, George was marvelling at the spectacle when out of the corner of his left eye he thought he saw three red dots travelling through the mist over the northern side of the ivy wall. Something stirred inside him. Could it be the ladybirds? Had they lured the butterflies out with the intention of harming them? He quietly flapped his wings and flew out.

The sun hadn't reached that side of the wall yet and the mist still lingered, thick and grey. George flew high, dipped low, circled around and strained his eyes, trying to see through the mist, but saw nothing. Seconds later, he heard distant muffled sounds. He stopped flapping and listened. It was only the whining of the wind blowing down from the northern hills.

"I've been seeing and hearing things," he moaned to

himself. He didn't feel like joining his friends this morning, so he flew farther away to Penny meadow.

***

"Lovely place you've got here, ladies," George said to a bunch of young ladybirds who were flying from one anemone to another. They weren't the five spot species. He counted their black dots.

"We mainly have small birds in our meadow," one of them said in a playful voice. "Crows rarely, and if they do come, they're always in pairs. You are alone then? You live on the rocks? on the hills?"

"I live in Blossom Valley. You may have heard of it," George replied.

They shook their heads.

"I have," shouted an older ladybird who was basking on a buttercup. "We had one from there, so she told us. She was a five spot species and gloating about it. Call me what you may, Crow, she looked a nasty piece of work, if you get my drift."

"Are the five spot ladybirds rare?" George asked.

"Thirteen and five spot ladybirds are very rare," the old ladybird answered. "We, here, are the seven spot species and, together with the ten spot, we are the most common ones, but we don't grumble. That's how nature made us. I'll tell you something I'm sure you don't know, Crow. Seven and ten spot ladybirds are bred in their millions and used for pest controlling purposes. We eat the flies, pests that damage the farmers' produce. So you see, Crow, all creatures have a purpose on this earth. Now, going back to what I was saying, this five spot took some of our own, lured them out, kept talking to them about Blossom Valley, some magical butterflies, a prince and a princess, and they followed her.

We never saw them again. Some days later, a sparrow, one of our regular visitors, asked me if we ladybirds can fly long distances and as high as birds can. I asked him why he wanted to know. He said he'd seen a number of them travelling towards the northern hills. He mentioned a place. Um, I'm not certain but I think I heard the word, *devil* something. *They were on their way to Blossom Valley*, I said to him. *What are you talking about, silly ladybird?* he asked mockingly. *There aren't any valleys up there, only steep ugly rocks.*"

"Did the sparrow say Devil's Gorge, ladybird?" George asked, anxiety mixed with fear in his voice.

"As I said, Crow, I don't remember. I wasn't paying much attention," the ladybird replied peevishly and moved away.

Devil's Gorge was a deep narrow passage with rough rock sides that fell deep down into a dry river. No trees or plants grew down there, only dead brambles, twisted and tangled up in massive heaps.

So why did Rosa take the ladybirds up there? What plan was in her devious mind? Why did the ladybirds never return to the meadow? What if my eyes and ears saw and heard right? What if Heather, as evil as her mother, has done the same with the butterflies?

Panic overtook him. Like an arrow he shot off into the sky. He was flying against the wind, its fierce gusts fighting furiously to send him reeling backwards, but he used all his might to give his wings the extra power and kept on flapping.

***

By now, Heather, her sisters and the butterflies were quite some distance away from Blossom Valley, and Heather was pleased her plan had gone well so far. No one had followed.

"Isn't it fun, girls?" she shouted in a cheerful voice. "I've waited a long time for a morning like this to take you out. Nobody saw us leave and nobody will know where we're going. I've planned to take you to a place you've never imagined, a place that will carry you away to another world. What do you say, Princess?"

"I say, what are we waiting for?" Princess Estella replied excitedly. Then, overcome by the sense of freedom, adventure and mischief, the butterflies giggled, danced, dipped and rose in the wind.

A short while later Heather's voice announced. "We're here, ladies, time to come down. We've landed safely on Devil's Gorge. I bet you've never flown to such heights before."

Estella had gone silent, turning her head left and right examining the surroundings. "I don't like this place," she said. "It's barren and bleak. The hills look menacing. Their jagged peaks look like scary ghosts, and the eerie moaning of this wind is giving me the creeps. I would much rather have gone to the meadows. We'd have fun there."

"Don't worry about the fun, Princess." Heather's mouth opened in a leering smirk. "We'll have plenty of that here. Now come and take a look at this magical plant of mine. It is unique and has powers that no one but I know."

Estella walked a few paces closer. The leaves of the plant were short and curly and its centre was a faint yellow. "Is this it?" she said with a frown. "That is but a plain weed with nothing magical about it and I am very disappointed you brought us up here to show us a weed. We're going back," she said firmly.

"No, you aren't," Heather retorted, a menacing look in her eyes. "I won't let you." Then she softened her voice and with a fake tone of concern went on. "I won't let you cause the flight is long as you've just experienced yourselves. The wind has picked up and will make the flight dangerous. I'd hate it if anything happened to you and we'd get the blame. We'll take you back. Don't get yourselves upset. Relax and let us have some fun. So, you called my unique plant a weed, didn't you, Princes? Ha! I'm going to prove to you that it isn't. You'll know how unique it is after you've taken a sniff from its yellow centre. Breathe long and deep, until your lungs are full. Straight away a wonderful feeling will travel through your body and mind and carry you away to a beautiful world."

Though Heather had spoken in a fake soft voice, there was malice in her eyes that she couldn't hide. The butterflies drew back and pulled Estella with them.

"Don't!" they whispered. "It's a trick. Heather is twisted. We mustn't trust her."

"Don't be silly," Estella whispered back. "It's only a plain weed. What harm can it do me?"

Without hesitating and with her usual grace and calmness, she walked to the weed, bent her head over its yellow centre and drew a deep breath. Seconds later, her eyes gleamed with tranquil joy.

"Come on, girls. Hurry up and join me," she called. "It's a wonderful sensation, you'll see."

The butterflies yielded and together bent over the weed and took deep breaths.

The power of the weed took over the butterflies' minds as if a spell had suddenly fallen on them and sent them into a trance. Imaginary plumes of haze swirled around them and inside those plumes, floated vague visions dancing to a soft tinkling sound. Estella beat at the haze to get it away from her eyes and she was now seeing fairies whirling and smiling at her.

"Stop turning and let me touch you," she pleaded. But the vision of the fairies gradually faded away, then vanished.

"They've gone," Estella whined drowsily. "Why?"

"They've gone cause they were never there, Princess." Heather said with a husky laugh. "It was an illusion that my magical plant created. And I'm not finished with you. The best is yet to come."

Heather's two sisters, who'd shrunk back terrified, now dared to come forward.

"Stop it, Heather!" Daisy, the older of the two, urged. "You're being cruel to them. Please stop."

"Clear off then!" Heather snarled. "I don't see why you fuss. It's only an innocent sleeping weed. The old owl nurse uses it to sooth her patients' pain or to sedate them if the injury is severe. Only she, being a nurse, knows how much she can give them. To delicate creatures like them, the effect…well, we'll have to wait and see. But it won't be the sleeping weed that'll kill them. I've been planning for a long time to get the butterflies out of the way, especially that one." She pointed at Estella and a spark of hatred and malevolence lit up her eyes.

"I've been up here before to put my plan to test. My mother does a lot of spying and learns secrets. Good job too, cause she heard Plato, the old owl, say that this sleeping weed is rare and only grows on Devil's Gorge. So she brought some meadow ladybirds, common worthless species, no one would miss."

"You've done this before?" Heather's two sisters gasped and drew back.

"I needed to test the power of the sleeping weed, didn't I? It had worked fine and so had the rest of my plan. I'm a genius like my mother. She planted the idea in my head. She stayed behind to see that Prince Orpheo has a long sleep so he can't alert the spider. A small dose of my magical weed will see to that. Now that you've heard it all, get out of my face or you won't live to see another day."

The butterflies wavered in the air for a second or two then dropped to the ground. They shuffled about letting out short sharp squeals and then went motionless.

Ten

Beaten by the wind, George's wings felt bruised and heavy as he landed on Devil's Gorge. His eyes blurry, he dragged his legs under a craggy bush and kept huffing and puffing and heaving until an urgent yell shook him.

"Don't, Heather, we beg you! Have mercy on them. They've done you no wrong. What's the matter with you? Have you no heart?"

George craned his neck and saw Heather darting across to her sisters.

"Keep your mouth shut," she hissed. "You'll wake them up. They're in a trance and must stay so until…You dare say another word and you'll be going the same way as them."

George stiffened. His eyes widened and his mouth gaped in utter disbelief. He tried to yell but his throat had frozen. Numb with horror, he watched Heather go back to the edge of the gorge and began speaking in a drawn-out, mesmeric voice.

"Now ladies, stand on your feet. Listen to my voice and obey its command. Take slow strides and come to me."

The butterflies did as the voice commanded and Heather moved aside.

"Good girls." she murmured deep in her throat. "Keep walking. You're almost there. Don't be afraid. It'll soon be over. Take one more stride and stay close together. Throw your heads forward. I'll be right behind you to help you take the leap to heaven."

With a fierce caw George whooshed out. "Stop evil creature! Stop!" he thundered and swept her away.

Heather jerked back violently and glared at him, her eyes blazing with fury.

"Treacherous black feathered creature!" she yelled. "How on earth did you find out? What evil spirit sent you to ruin my plan? Go to hell! Get out of my sight! Get out!" She screamed on and on with bitterness outrage and madness until she had no more voice left to scream and then she collapsed with a venomous hiss.

Another split second and the butterflies would fall over the edge to their death. They were standing right on the edge. George couldn't save them from behind. A sudden sound or movement might startle them and send them toppling over. He had to be at the front so he could look at them and talk to them. "Oh God, help me!" he panted. He noticed some tufts of grass sprouting out of the rock crevice and clawed on them. George lashed his wings against the rock and yelled, "wake up Princess! Wake up, all of you and step back! Step back! Help! Help!"

The butterflies didn't move. They stared at him and the look in their eyes was distant and cloudy.

George's heart sank and his eyes filled with tears. "Move back, Princess Estella," he cried helplessly. The butterflies staggered slightly backwards and through his tears, George saw a slow blink in their eyes. Encouraged, he cried. Help! Help!"

A horde of bumblebees that happened to be a short flight away, responded to his cries. One flew over to him while the others moved the dazed butterflies away from the edge.

"A pretty mess you've got yourself into, haven't you, Crow? What happened?"

George hadn't seen such a stout bumblebee before. She had a pretty face and her eyes shone with kindness.

"Gloria's my name. Call me Glo. How can we help?"

"Take care of the butterflies. Keep talking to them until they come round. Heather forced them to sniff the sleeping weed. It will take time to wear off. Keep them safe. Don't let that wicked ladybird get away. Her sisters are innocent. Send a message to Plato the owl. Any creature will know him, but hurry!"

"Don't worry, Crow, I know the old owl well. Concentrate on getting yourself out of the plight you're in."

"I don't think that I can," he said. "These tufts have gone loose under my grip and I can't use my wings; they're bruised and…"

Before he could say any more, he felt the grass slipping away. With the last bit of strength he had, he tried to scramble up, scraping his claws on the hard rock surface, and in his despair he pulled hard on the tufts of grass which came away at the roots. Damp soil, landed on his chest and sent him plummeting onto the thorny bed of the brambles. As he lay flat on his back, wings spread out, he tossed and turned to free himself from the thorns, but they'd snagged deep in his feathers and were tearing his flesh. He gave up the struggle, let out a deep moan of pain and shut his eyes.

The bumble bees peered down and squeaked with dread when they saw the blood oozing from his sides.

"He's dead," one of them cried.

***

With the help of the bumblebees, the butterflies came round, feeling giddy, weak and tired, but remembered nothing of their nasty ordeal. When Glo was confident they were fit for the long flight, some of her girls escorted them back to Blossom Valley.

While the bumblebees were busy attending to the butterflies, Heather shambled about in a thick clump of grass, stunned at the unexpected turn of events, and for the first time ever she allowed tears to run down her face.

After all her hard work, the months of planning and experimenting, her dream of getting rid of the butterflies had been wrecked. Heck, she'd come so close! One more instant and it would have been over. Those precious butterflies would have gone forever, perished on the sharp thorns of the brambles and no one would have known. It would have been hers and her mother's secret. Her two so-called-sisters, who in fact were two strays her mother had picked up, wouldn't make it back to Blossom Valley. She'd planned something clever which would make it look as if they were the ones who had taken the butterflies out but had never made it back. They would go the same way as the butterflies and perish on the brambles. The winds would blow their remains, if there were any, away across the hills. She would then sneak back into the valley and spread the story that her two young sisters had told her they were taking the butterflies out to the cornfields for the day and had asked her to keep it a secret. A huge search would take place, the whole valley looking for the butterflies. She and her mother would be looking for the young sisters, calling their names, searching under trees and bushes and laughing silently to themselves. Their disappearance would remain a mystery for many years to come and she and her mother would have the last laugh. They'd be the happiest creatures on earth to see the spider mourn her precious Estella and the rare butterflies. And Orpheo oh, how she'd love to see him grieve for his princess! She would be there to comfort him. Of course she would. In time his wound would heal and he'd come to like her, love her and marry her. Heck! Heck! She wept, if it weren't for that damned crow. He's now lying dead on the thorns, but what good has that done her.

She peered through the grass blades and saw her sisters clinging to each other, weeping and an idea struck her. She cautiously walked over to them. "You must help me escape," she said.

"How? " The young ladybirds asked.

"Wipe your stupid tears, put on a better face and walk slowly to where the bumblebees are. Try to distract them by talking to them, asking questions about the gorge or whatever. Don't try anything funny. Remember you'll have to face my mother if anything happens to me. Now start moving."

The two sisters did as they were told and, chatting cheerfully, they reached the bumblebees.

"Hello girls," Glo said loudly. "We're glad to see you look well. You want some company, don't you?"

"We would like to ask you some questions about the gorge, if you have the time."

"We have all the time in the world, girls," said Gloria her eyes darting in all directions, recording the slightest movements all around and at the same time communicating with her girls with a series of peculiar barely-audible hissing sound that she made through her half closed lips.

Heather looked around. Her sisters were doing a good job she thought, because Glo, the fearsome bumblebee seemed quite relaxed, sharing a joke with the young ladybirds, but she couldn't see that Glo's eyes were still recording movements and her half shut mouth was still emitting those peculiar hissing signals.

Heather opened her wing shell. But before she let her wings out, three huge bumblebees pounced on her from behind.

"Oh no, you don't!" shouted Glo and held her shell tight.

"Let go of me!" Heather screamed, pushing and kicking to free herself. "I was only trying to stretch my wings a bit, that's all."

"Ha! Ha!" Glo scoffed. "Nice try. You thought you'd fool us, you ghastly creature.

We've kept our eyes and ears on you in our secret way the whole time. We heard what you said to your sisters. Tie her wings shell, girls. That'll keep her nice and still."

"No, you don't!" Heather screamed. "I won't let you ruin, my five spot shell, you ugly fat monsters."

Glo's eyes flashed with anger. "You were about to kill those innocent butterflies in a most cruel way and you think I should give a damn about your shell? Put her in the wicker basket, girls. Keep the young sisters separate," she whispered. "They took no part in any of this, the crow told me."

Eleven

The strong winds had snatched George's cries and sent their quavering echoes across the woods and plains. Up in his tree Plato stirred when the first echo travelled though Penny Wood. He listened. There came a second, then a third.

"A crow's cries," Plato muttered.

Immediately he let out his alarm hoot and Swift, the scout bird, responded in no time.

"I heard the cries." Swift said. "I gauged their direction. They came from over there."

"That's the direction of Devil's Gorge," Plato replied. "There isn't much life up there. What could have happened?"

"I was on my way to investigate when I heard your call. I'm certain it was a crow's cries for help."

"Swift," Plato said urgently. "Send Nurse Tawny Owl over there. The ambulance cart must take the short cut behind the hospital. Tell the hares. They'll know which route I mean. Avoid talking to anyone, even Thelma. Otherwise panic will spread throughout the valley."

Swift nodded and in the blink of an eye he'd disappeared into the clouds.

Plato sped through the air in eerie silence but after he'd left the woods and plains behind, the strong gusts of the northerly wind, came racing against him whipping his wings and snatching the air from his lungs. He blinked trying to see through his clouded eyes, but could make out nothing. He dropped to the ground and regained his breath. He dried his eyes and looked around to make sure the wind hadn't drifted him off course.

"Plato!" exclaimed Gloria. "I flew out to see whether you were coming. I knew you'd pick up the cries and was certain you'd come. Am I glad to see you, old, friend!"

"What on earth are you doing up here, Gloria?" Plato said in puzzlement.

"I've got my girls with me," she replied. "There's no time to tell everything but, in a nut shell, the ladybird tried to kill the butterflies. The crow saved them but is now lying on the brambles, as good as dead."

Plato swallowed hard to get rid of the lump that suddenly wedged into his throat. "Let us make haste, Gloria," he said. "We're only a short flight away."

Plato's eyes filled with grief as he hovered over George's still body. Trying to avoid the sharp thorns, Plato landed beside the crow and bent over his chest but he couldn't tell if there was a heartbeat there.

"George, can you hear me?" he cried, his face right beside George's. "Hold on, my friend! Help, is arriving. Can you hear me?"

But the crow's eyes remained shut tight and his body stiff.

"Has he got a pulse? Did you check?" were Tawny Owl's words before she'd even landed.

Plato looked up. "I couldn't find any. I hope I'm wrong but I thought his body was slightly warm if that means anything."

Tawny Owl, her face marked with anxiety, hovered over George's body.

"The thorns look ominous," she said gravely. "He's lost a lot of blood. His back must be stitched straight away or he won't last and it could already be too late. I can't do it down there, Plato. I'm going to fetch the reel of vine I always keep in the ambulance. There's no other way but to haul him up." With that she was gone.

For a few short seconds Plato remained sceptical, his mind working fast, weighing up the options.

"Hauling him up won't do," he said loudly to himself. "The thorns will pull on his feathers and tear the skin. No time to consider any other option but to act now, for every fraction of a second is precious."

At once he set his strong beak to work, hacking at the dry thorns. With great speed he went as far under George's body as possible and under his wings. After he had freed both wings, he folded them across George's chest and went on clearing a big patch he could steady himself on. Next, he curled his talons under George's body and beat his wings hard to give them power. He slowly lifted up and up, inch by inch, until finally he reached the top and lay George's body on the stretcher.

"Do your best, Tawny Owl," he gasped breathlessly.

The bumblebees, the ambulance hares and even Tawny Owl who'd been watching on tenterhooks heaved sighs of relief.

Before she turned George on his tummy, Tawny Owl forced his beak open and squeezed a couple of drops of some thick liquid in. She then washed away the blood and, taking great care, she stitched the torn skin. She spread another kind of jelly on his back and took him to the ambulance which drawn by the four special hares zoomed out of sight.

Plato fixed his eyes on Tawny Owl, waiting for her to speak.

"George is gravely ill," she began. "He's lost a lot of blood. I've given him something that hopefully will steady his weak heart beat until he and I can get to the hospital. He may not make it, Plato, I must warn you. His wings are badly bruised and a number of the finer bones on his back are fractured though they may heal with time. What mostly worries me is his mental state. He suffered a horrific shock today and not so long ago he went through the trauma of seeing his parents shot, followed by the fire at Crow Lake. He's been through a lot of emotional suffering, Plato. He will need the best attention and medical care, which of course he will get. I only pray to God that he stays with us. Thelma needs to know. I trust that you'll tell her as soon as you get to the valley."

Tawny Owl beat her wings and in the next instant she was speeding across the sky.

Plato sat pensive, lost in sorrowful thoughts, his eyes staring into empty space. It was Glo who shook him out of his thoughts. "George is strong and determined, he'll pull through you'll see," she said with a smile. "The butterflies should be safely in Blossom Valley by now. We'll leave it to you to tell Thelma what happened. Heather is securely cooped up in the wicker basket. The young ones who did no wrong, the crow told me before, he…" – she hesitated – "we kept them separate. We'll bring them over in a while. Give the ambulance cart time to reach the hospital and Tawny Owl a chance to see to George."

"You're very thoughtful and kind, Gloria," Plato said. "All of you are and we are very grateful. I hope you'll stay in Blossom Valley for a while. I'm sure you'll want to know how George is doing." He nodded his head in farewell and rose in the air.

Twelve

The butterflies apologised to Thelma and wept for George who had put his life in danger to save theirs. But for Thelma, no matter how hard she tried the chilling thought that she nearly lost them stayed at the back of her mind and kept creeping out to trouble her. The glory of the lost kingdom would be reborn, and the butterflies had to be there to carry on the legend. She knew this, for she was there when the evil force had fallen upon them. Winters had piled upon winters and springs upon springs since then. She'd been counting the cuckoo's spring messages. Not long to go before the butterflies, and her, were rid of the horrific evil.

The bumblebees had brought cheer to the valley and everybody loved them and the bumblebees in turn loved them back. Together with the other creatures they spent hours on the hospital forecourt waiting for news about George. Many wanted to visit him, but each time, Tawny Owl would step out on the forecourt to say that George was stable but not fit enough to see visitors. Besides her, only Plato and Thelma knew that George had fallen into a coma and the chances of him pulling out of it were slim.

A whole few days passed and again Tawny Owl came out onto the broad hospital step. The forecourt swarmed with creatures and all eyes rested on her face.

"I appreciate your eagerness to learn about George's recovery," she said, "and so will he when he's better. But right now you are not helping by camping out here. On the contrary, the noise might disturb him and the other patients as well. George's recovery is slow but steady. He's weak and needs rest. So I urge you to go home now and when George is fit enough, he'll come out and say hello to you all."

The creatures, sad and disheartened, trooped silently downhill, and Conti, his head drooping with weariness, his brow furrowing with thought, fell in line beside them. But before the path wound round some tall bushes, Conti dropped back, turned sharply to his left and took a shortcut back to the hospital. He wasn't prepared to wait another day to hear Tawny Owl going over the same excuses. He needed to see George now. He had to tell him his dream before his brain deleted it.

A rabbit, bolting in long hops, suddenly shot his way.

"Shush! What are you doing on this path?" Conti whispered.

"I was going to ask you the same question. This is a rabbit run. So what are you doing on a rabbit run, Frog?" The rabbit gazed at him suspiciously.

"Mm…err! Oh, dear me, I must have got lost. Thanks for telling me, Rabbit," Conti said with a teasing twinkle in his eyes.

He hid behind a tree, waited for a couple of minutes then hopped on. The moon hadn't shown up yet and the sky was empty of stars. He searched round the hospital for a way in. All doors were locked. Only a small window higher up was ajar. He gathered rocks from a rockery nearby and made a solid heap of them. He hopped on it and took a huge leap but fell flat on the ground. But after numerous attempts he managed to get himself onto the window ledge and jumped inside.

The moon had now come out and was sitting on top of the elm tree. Strips and speckles of its pale yellow light came through the windows and lit the corridor.

The first door on his right was ajar and he peered in. He saw two rabbits. Each had one leg on a sling suspended from the ceiling and both were snoring away. There was a third rabbit in a corner bed. His right leg was in plaster and he was groaning in his sleep.

In the room next door was a squirrel, his head swathed in white bandage. He was awake, staring at the ceiling, muttering a verse from the *Good Night Song*.

Further down, a young hedgehog, both legs in plaster, was sobbing loudly. Conti hopped in.

"Hush, hush young fellow," he whispered. "Are you in pain?"

"No, I'm not. I want my mummy," the hedgehog cried.

"I'll fetch your mummy if you stop crying." Conti gently stroked his forehead. "Close your eyes and sleep… sleep."

"I want a story first," the young fellow whined.

"I'm not a good storyteller but what would you say if I sang you a lullaby instead?"

"Okay, then. It better be a good one," said the hedgehog with a sigh and burrowed deep under his blanket.

Rocking his bed gently, Conti used his softest, sweetest voice and sang *Rock-a- bye baby on the tree top*, until he'd lulled him to sleep. Then he tiptoed out and pulled the door behind him.

There was one room left to open but the door was tightly shut. He fumbled at the handle, then pressed it down and walked in. Some speckles of yellow light fell on a small bed and a black head stuck out from under a white blanket. Conti's heart thudded in his chest as he came closer. It was George, lying on his side, his head turned towards the wall. There was a stool at the other side of the bed and Conti leapt on it.

"If Tawny Owl finds me here I'll be in big trouble, George," he whispered, "but I don't care cause I couldn't wait another day. I've been bursting to tell you the dream I had the other night. You were in it, George. You sound as if you're fast asleep cause your breathing is light but I can't trust my brain will keep it much longer, so I'm going to tell you now.

I was in the Opera House with my tenor, you know the one. He was the main character and I was the support one and I can tell you, George, I was good, I was." Conti puffed himself out and his face lit up with pride. "When the curtain fell, George, they cheered me, they did. But before I left the stage a voice, a single voice, rose from amongst the crowd. Bravo! Bravo! I looked, and there, on a blue velvet seat, third row up, I saw you, buddy, clapping and shouting, *Bravo Conti*!"

George stirred and let out a muffled groan.

"Did I wake you, George? Sorry. I didn't mean to."

"You've been talking to the back of my neck all this time. Come round so I can see you," George said, moaning with pain.

Conti pulled the stool to the other side and jumped on it.

"What's *buddy*? That's a new word I've never heard."

"It's friend. Buddy means friend. My tenor used to call me that, and you're my best friend, George, didn't you know? Well, I'm telling you, you're the best buddy in the whole wide world."

"Thank you, buddy." George tried to laugh. "Aah! Aah!" He flinched. "The stitches are pulling me something rotten."

Suddenly, the young hedgehog started to cry. "Mummy... mummy..."

Tawny Owl rushed in. The other patients woke up, remembered their pain and started moaning and groaning loudly.

"What's the matter, young patient? Tell Tawny Owl where it hurts and she'll make it better."

"I want my mummy," the little fellow whimpered. "The frog promised to fetch her. Where is he?"

"Your mummy will be here in the morning and the frog is in his pond."

"No he isn't. He was here. He sang me a lullaby. I know what I'm talking about, and no, I wasn't dreaming. He lied to me. Wait until I get out of here. I'll…"

Tawny Owl gave him a few drops of syrup and sat at his bedside, tenderly stroking his brow until he was fast asleep.

As she came out on the corridor, she heard whispering voices coming from George's room.

"The frog…" she muttered. "That little fellow was telling the truth." She opened the door and stood in the doorway. "Why are you here, Conti? Didn't I say…" Her voice was stern and her eyes scowling.

"Sorry, I didn't mean to wake him…err…I…Did I do something terrible, Tawny Owl?"

"Did you wake him up?" She gasped trying to hide her joy. Then she took a good look at George and her whole face lit up.

"Good to have you back, George," she said gently. "Hope your stitches aren't hurting you badly. I'll see to them straight away. Only give me two ticks."

She flew up onto the hospital roof and let out a short hoot and a second later Plato glided down beside her.

"I was already down. I've spent part of each night in the hospital grounds. So tell me the news," he said, not daring to look at her face.

"Brilliant news, Plato, thanks to the frog who managed to pull him out of the coma!"

"I can't tell you how relieved I am, Tawny Owl." Plato breathed in and let the air slowly out. "I dreaded that George might not pull through. Did you give him…?"

"I will give him a drop of your master's remedy straight away and you can visit him in a couple of days. But remember my warning about his mental state. Do not stress him with unnecessary questions."

Conti was outside the hospital entrance waiting for Tawny Owl. "I expect you want me out of your way, don't you, Tawny Owl?" he asked. "But there's something baffling me and my brain can't figure it out. You said, *It's good to have you back, George.* Where had George gone then? Had he gone away?"

Tawny Owl's eyes filled with amusement.

"He'd gone into a coma, which is a medical word for a very, very deep sleep and for a very, very long time. It can happen to wild creatures like us and to the humans. Nothing to trouble your brain with, Conti, I'm very glad you woke him."

Thirteen

George was limping across the room, when Plato visited him two days later.

"George!" Plato called.

"Hello, Plato, I'm testing my strength. I don't know what potion Tawny Owl has been giving me but it's working wonders with me already. The pain has eased and I feel brighter. I reckon I'll be good as new soon and, Plato, you saved my life. Tawny Owl told me. Thank you. How are the butterflies?"

"They're fine and so are the bumblebees. They like it here and they've decided to stay on." Then Plato turned serious. "The ladybirds' trial will take place tomorrow. Thelma wants it over and done with before the spring celebration. You're still very frail, George, but I ought to ask you: do you want to attend the trial?"

He stared at George, waiting for his answer, and in his eyes Plato saw that the terror was still with him and he wished he hadn't asked. George's body suddenly shook and as the horrific scenes on the gorge flashed across his mind, his eyes turned wild and husky screams came out of his mouth. "No! No!" Then he went still, staring at the blank wall.

A worried-looking Tawny Owl rushed in. Shaking her head, she gave Plato a long scowling glare that said. *You ignored my warning.*

"I didn't mean to upset you, George. It was thoughtless of me. I'm sorry," Plato said regretfully.

66

"You don't have to apologise, Plato," George said and came to stand in front of him. "I can't bring myself to even look at that evil creature, let alone be in the Hall with her."

There was a light tap on the door and Thelma peered inside.

"Thelma!" George exclaimed. "It's good of you to come." His wild eyes had softened and a calmer expression spread across his face.

"It's good to see you're on the mend, George," she said. "Everyone is wishing you well and hopes to see you out and about soon."

Plato fixed her with a glance and immediately Thelma grasped its meaning. "Tawny Owl will be starting her hospital round any minute now, so it's time we went, George. We'll see you again soon," she said and followed Plato out of the room.

**

The trial would be held at the Music Hall. As it was too small to hold every single creature of Blossom Valley, the head of each family would pick twelve adult members of mixed gender. They were told what tier they would be sitting in and that disciplined behaviour should be observed at all times.

When the double doors of the Music Hall were thrown open, the creatures entered in orderly fashion and took their places. On the top tier sat the members of all the bird families. In the next tier down sat the squirrels, rabbits and hedgehogs, then the ants, Speedo the snail and next to him, Conti the frog. On the first tier sat Thelma and Orpheo, the butterfly prince, then Gloria the bumblebee and her girls. On the far right of the row, tight-lipped, and stormy-faced sat Rosa, the ladybird. The butterflies were kept at the ant village where a number of magpies where scattered on the ground, and in the trees and bushes to guard their safety.

On the small stage of the Music Hall stood a desk with a high chair behind it where the judge, Plato the owl, was seated.

Stony-faced, wings folded across his chest, Plato stared towards the entrance as the guards, two stout magpies, brought the ladybirds in. Everyone up in the seats craned their necks and tilted their heads left and right to get a good view of them as they stood to face the judge. Heather stood at the front, one guard on either side of her, and her young sisters stood behind. Plato rested his stern eyes on Heather and spoke.

"Ladybird Heather, you are here to be tried for the wicked deed you committed. You cunningly lured the innocent, gullible butterflies out onto Devil's Gorge with the intention of killing them, but not before you put them through a terrifying ordeal. George the crow, with the bumblebees' help, saved the butterflies from a cruel death. Sadly, George can't be here to tell us what happened as he's been very ill in hospital because of you. The bumblebees saw enough, but it is you and your sisters who know exactly what took place on the gorge, and we are ready to listen."

"The bumblebees treated us horribly," Heather shrieked, casting a hate-filled glare at Glo. "We did nothing wrong, we were playing a game and having fun."

"Describe to us, Ladybird Heather, the game you were playing that was such great fun," Plato demanded.

"Hold on," Rosa blurted out. "My daughter told you, you play a game to have fun. A game is a game and we all know what fun is. What more do you want?"

"The question is not for you, to answer Rosa, so sit down please," Plato said in a calm but commanding voice.

"No, I won't," Rosa snarled. "And you, learned judge that you are, have a duty to listen and take note to what the defence tells you. Firstly, my Heather is a kind being. She can be loud and rough at times, but she means no harm. Secondly, I never allowed my daughters to fly outside the valley. I don't know where Devil's Gorge is, so how would any of my daughters know? You, you know-all owl, should know that ladybirds, especially us five spot species, don't fly to such heights as only birds can reach. It was the crow who led the butterflies out on the gorge. My daughters simply followed. Once there, he coaxed them into playing games while he hid in the bushes. What he had in mind was to come out and kill them. Why? Cause he's evil. All crows are. Witches' best mates," she hissed through closed lips.

It did not straightaway dawn on the creatures that the crow Rosa was talking about was George and they looked at one another with a confused expression in their eyes.

Plato choked up with horror and it took him a while before he could get the words out of his mouth. "What did you say?"

"What? … What?" the crows yelled their eyes widening in total disbelief. "Does she mean it was George?" Then an outburst of raging carks shook the entire Hall. "Get her out of here," the crows kept carking.

"Chuck her out!" the blackbirds and sparrows protested in deafening whooping cries.

The din roared inside Plato's head and sent it spinning. He rubbed his temples and took long calming breaths.

"Order, Order! Everyone!" he shouted.

After the din had died down, the creatures lapsed into dismal silence. The rabbits, sensitive to this kind of behaviour, were gripped by continuous snuffles and tears, but stopped as everyone gave them funny looks. Afterwards, they scratched their ears until they bled, then groaned with pain. The red squirrels snorted, darting their heads up and down left and right non- stop. The hedgehogs gawked at the squirrels then rolled up on their seats and did not move. The ants let out a series of tiny grunts and Speedo the snail stared at Conti next to him then gave a quivering shrill cry and scooted into his shell. Conti the frog, eyes bulging out of his head, sat chewing on his tongue jabbering. All of a sudden he jumped up like a jack-in-the- box and, still jabbering, took some huge leaps over the seats and landed in front of Plato. He rolled his cloudy eyes and spluttered. "You, of all creatures Plato, shouldn't allow her to tell such sickening lies about George. Kick her out at once!"

"Kick her out, Kick her out!" All the creatures stood up and joined in.

"Please be quiet! You too, Conti," Plato ordered.

"No, I won't," Conti croaked stubbornly, "cause George is my buddy and I know he wouldn't hurt a dead fly. He's the kindest creature in the whole wide world." His head drooping and tears rolling down his cheeks, Conti hopped back to his seat.

There fell a spell of gloomy silence until Rosa's screechy voice filled the hall. "Ask the crow. Go on, ask him. But you can't, can you, Owl? cause he can't speak. He's in a coma which means he's as good as dead." She curled her lips into a sly grin. "I know, cause nothing escapes me. I heard the old owl nurse tell you. The crow is going to die and whatever he saw out there will go with him to his grave."

"Heinous ladybird! " Plato's voice echoed across the hall. "Guard your tongue or leave at once."

"I'm not done yet," she grunted and carried on. "The bumblebees flew there cause they heard the crow yelling at the butterflies and heard my poor Heather screaming with fright. When they realised the crow was about to kill them, they stung him on the neck to numb him then pushed him over the edge and onto the brambles. Now you've got the whole picture of what happened on the gorge and I'm done."

There wasn't a single cough, whisper or shuffle in the hall. They all sat rigid on their seats, gobsmacked and horror stricken.

Conti hopped quietly onto the tier above his and tapped Bond the red squirrel on his back.

"Hear, hear!" he whispered. "George isn't in a coma. He was, but he's awake now and recovering. My buddy isn't going to die. Pass it on to the crows and tell them to keep it to themselves and, if you want to know what a coma is, it's when we fall into a very deep sleep and can't wake up. Tawny Owl explained it to me. I was at his bedside, determined to tell him the dream I had. He was in it, and I reckon that did it. My dream pulled him out of his coma. Tawny Owl was very happy that I did."

After a short and dismal silence, Plato coughed to clear his throat and spoke.

"Ladybird Rosa, You've been defending your daughter for some few minutes now. You described scenes that took place on Devil's Gorge in detail, as if you were there. But you weren't, were you, ladybird Rosa? We have witnesses who on that morning saw you inside the valley, moving secretively about and, to speak more plainly, lurking around the butterflies' pen."

"I was on the gorge, not inside the valley," Rosa shrieked.

"Liar, Liar!" Glo shouted. "How come we didn't see you up there? Liar! You're not only poisonous and vile, you're sick in the head." She filled her cheeks with air, let it out with a loud whistling sound and flew at Rosa.

"Bumblebee Gloria, return to you seat please," Plato ordered. "We do not allow violent behaviour during a trial. Solve your differences outside the hall."

There was a short pause before Plato spoke again.

"Will Heather's sister come to the front, please?"

A pretty ladybird, her wings shell a glossy red, lowered her head in a polite bow. "I'm Daisy," she said, "and behind me is my younger sister Po…"

"Be careful Daisy, my treasure," Rosa blurted out in a softened voice. "Don't let the old owl lead you on. You must protect your sister, our Heather."

The young ladybird looked right into Plato's eyes, her voice steady and clear now and repeated. "I'm Daisy, and behind me is my younger sister, Poppy, and we are not Rosa's daughters. Heather is, and she did it. She and her mother plotted the whole thing. Heather had tried the hypnotic power of the sleeping weed on some meadow ladybirds. It had worked, she told us. The meadow ladybirds, who she called common and worthless, had gone over the edge of the gorge and perished in the brambles. She was jealous of the butterflies' beauty and loathed Thelma for the way she fawned over them. She did some dreadful things to the butterflies. We begged her to stop and she threatened to kill us, didn't she, Poppy?"

Poppy couldn't utter a word.

"Poppy?" her sister demanded.

"She did," Poppy stammered. "We're sorry we couldn't stop her…" The young ladybird choked on her tears and sat down.

"You ungrateful creatures," Rosa said, breaking into fake hysterics. "After all I've done for you, is this how you repay me?" She buried her face in her hands and sobbed on and on.

"Yes it is," Daisy answered firmly. "You told us we were strays and a merciful being that you were you'd take care of us. Instead, all you gave us was fear and punishment." Then Daisy broke down with emotion.

Sadness gripped the silent Music Hall. Only Conti's loud sniffles and hiccups could be heard. Plato let out a long sigh and, standing up, spoke in a sombre voice. "Fellow creatures, are you ready to give your judgement?"

"Yes we are," they shouted.

"Only the head of each family will answer my question. Do you judge the ladybirds Daisy and Poppy to be innocent or guilty?"

"Innocent!" shouted the family heads at the top of their voices.

"Do you judge Ladybird Heather to be innocent or guilty?"

"Guilty!"

The entire hall rocked as all the creatures stood up yelling angrily, "Guilty! Guilty! Guilty!"

"Thank you," Plato called. "Please seat down." Then he fixed his gaze upon Heather, searching for signs of remorse, but what he saw in her eyes was malice, darkness and ill will that seemed to be coming from deep inside her.

"Ladybird Heather," he said, "you have been found guilty of a dreadful deed, and for this reason you are banished from Blossom Valley. You'll be taken far beyond the hills and plains, so far that you'll never find your way back. Guards, take her away."

"Liars, liars…!" Rosa raved. "What's banishment, huh? You're going to kill her. Say it clearly. Murderers! You'll kill my beautiful daughter, and you"- her searing eyes stopped at Thelma – "you, wretched spider, listen to my words cause you'll hear them only once. I vow revenge on you and your precious butterflies." Foam flecked the corners of her mouth and her eyes blazed with such raging hatred that Thelma shrank back, shivering.

While Heather was shrieking, pushing and kicking to wrench herself free from the guards, Rosa stormed out of the hall. She filled her lungs with gulps of fresh air then hid under a nearby cluster of bluebells.

Fourteen

When the Music Hall had emptied, and all the talk and whispers had died away, Rosa came out of hiding. She checked the trees, bushes and the sky above for she feared the crows might avenge George and all the crows she'd called evil. She squirmed through a gap in the ivy and into the undergrowth outside the northern wall. She took a few long breaths and let herself sail in the gentle wind until she reached the meadow. There, she rested on the blossoms of a wild cherry tree and looked around.

A cluster of meadow ladybirds flew onto the branch next to her and one spoke. "You are a stranger in these parts, aren't you? What meadow have you come from?"

"Five spot ladybirds don't live in meadows," Rosa snapped and turned round so they could see her vivid black spots. "We're rare. There are very few of us about."

The words *five spot* and *rare* rang a bell with the old ladybird who'd been peacefully napping on a meadow orchid. She jerked awake and flew over. She had questions that needed answers.

"Oi, I remember you! So, why are you lying? Your arrogance and gloating has given you away. You took some of our girls, didn't you? Where are they?"

"I didn't take them. They begged me to let them come with me to Blossom Valley and I did. They were awed by the beauty of the place and the butterflies, especially the prince and princess. Aren't they back?" she asked with fake concern in her voice.

"No, they never returned."

"And is this my fault? They could have drifted elsewhere unless…"

"What do you mean unless?" the old ladybird demanded.

"The spider, who is the head of the creatures there, has a thing against ladybirds. So she probably killed them. I can't think of anything else."

"What were they doing in the air if they'd been killed then? cause our sparrow friend and permanent resident here told us he saw ladybirds flying towards the northern rocks, and sparrows' eyes miss nothing that goes on in the sky. Did you take them there?" The old ladybird glared at her suspiciously.

"No dear," Rosa said mockingly. "I didn't. They wanted to see Blossom Valley, not Devil's Gorge."

"Hold it, hold it right there, for I'm smelling something very suspicious here. How come you know that Devil's Gorge is on the northern rocks if you've never been there?"

Anger boiled inside Rosa for she'd never been cornered like this before, and anger loosened her tongue. "You're more stupid than you look," she snorted. "But I shouldn't expect any better from a common empty-headed meadow ladybird. The answer to your question is plain. Now watch my lips as the words will be coming out one by one. I have heard the big birds talk about the Devil's Gorge and Blossom Valley, the place where I live, has hundreds of them, happy, now?"

Straight away Rosa was mad at herself and that was rare for she realized she'd gone too far, replying to the old ladybird with such very insulting words. Meadow ladybirds could come in useful. They might even be the answer to her problem. This was the reason she was here. Stupid and worthless they were, but they had strong jaws that could snap a delicate butterfly's neck with little effort.

"I didn't mean to be rude," she apologised hastily. "I'm very sorry if I have offended you. I can't think straight. They've killed my daughters." She pretended she was choking with emotion. "They killed my three angels."

The young ladybirds, interested in any piece of news or gossip that came from beyond the meadow, gathered around her.

"Who killed your daughters? Why?"

"It's a long story. It's best that I start from the beginning," she said with a sigh.

"We lived in the Abbey gardens and were very happy there, until they opened the place to the humans. Then I kept losing my young ones. Children took them away in glass jars and it was happening all the time. It left me heartbroken. I'd heard of Blossom Valley. I took my three daughters and moved there, hoping for a better life. But the damn spider, the head of all the creatures there, made our life hell. She wouldn't let my daughters mix with her butterflies. As I said, the spider has a thing against us ladybirds. My daughters were blamed and punished for any trivial misdoing, even if it were an accident. A small accident took place the other day. The butterflies weren't hurt. Only a crow who happened to be close by got in a bit of trouble and slightly injured himself. My daughters got the blame for it, and the spider banished them from Blossom Valley. But she can't fool me. She snatched the opportunity to get rid of them and kill them." Rosa burst out in loud sobs. "I want to see justice done."

The old ladybird wasn't touched by Rosa's sobbing story.

"So," she said, "I suppose you want to see the spider punished, dead perhaps?"

"No, I want her precious butterflies dead. The spider must live to grieve and suffer for their loss, like I'll be doing for my daughters for the rest of my living days. I know of a good and tested way to get rid of them but I can't do it alone."

"So you want us to help you kill the butterflies who have never done you wrong? That's ghastly, cruel and appalling. How dare you ask such a thing from us? Go away and never…"

Just then, the leaves and dry twigs on the ground rustled and a husky voice spoke. "Excuse us for barging in on you like this, ladies, we are…"

"I know who you are," Rosa snapped. " A gang of bedraggled grasshoppers on the run."

"Bedraggled we might be, for we've travelled far, but I can assure you, lady, we're not on the run."

The ladybirds glared at Rosa then at the grasshopper and flew away in disgust.

The grasshopper introduced himself. "I'm Gaspar, the leader of this team."

His gang stayed well back, half-smiles on their faces.

"I couldn't help overhearing the sad story you told the ladybirds and I thought I might be able to help."

Rosa took a few paces closer and gave Gaspar a long stare. His face was scarred in more than one place and his eyes were swollen, as if he'd been struck by a nasty blow.

"So," Gaspar continued, "you believe your daughters were unfairly punished?"

"I believe, if the truth be known, that my daughters are dead," Rosa answered. "The spider made sure of that and I want to pay her back."

"Hmmm…It is revenge you're after, and who can blame you?" He paced up and down, stroking his forehead.

"Well, lady," he said with a sly grin, "you might be in luck cause my brain has just come up with a brilliant idea. Shall I call you lady, or you have a name?"

"It's Rosa," she said drily then fell silent, pondering. Grasshoppers were the last creatures she would turn to for help at the best of times. On the other hand, they were strong, ruthless and cunning. She had nothing to lose by listening to his so-called brilliant idea. She cleared her throat and asked, "What's this brilliant idea of yours? And anyway what means could a grasshopper have…"

"Ha!" Gaspar interrupted. Holding his head up, he paced up and down as if he were somebody of great importance. "I'll tell you what means I have Rosa. I'm a well-known and highly respected creature. You don't know me cause you're a mere newcomer to these parts. I have many connections, friends, if you know what I mean. I have great power over them and can persuade them to go along with any cleverly thought-out idea of mine."

"I don't want to listen to fancy talk and big ideas, for they count for nothing," Rosa said in an ice-cold voice. "I want facts. Who are these friends of yours then? Tell me."

"It's not for you to worry your pretty little head over," he replied. "I can't tell you much at this stage. I do things properly, me. I think before I plan and never make plans before I investigate. But I can tell you this much. My friends, or mates as I call them, are powerful, ferocious and stubborn creatures capable of causing great damage. Now you tell me about Blossom Valley. What is it like?"

"Well," she began, "it's a vast place and very beautiful but everyone there is very hostile. There's Thelma, a ghastly enormous spider who's the boss of pretty much everything and everybody. The butterflies, and I admit they're very beautiful, especially the prince and his princess. There's a wrinkly old frog who croaks non- stop and drives you crazy. Then the ant colonies, thousands of these horrible midgets that give me the creeps."

At the mention of the word *ants* a spark flickered across Gaspar's eyes. He turned and winked at his gang.

"And the birds…" Rosa paused, as she noticed Gaspar's slit eyes widen with apprehension. She realised she'd slipped up. Birds were the grasshoppers' dreaded enemy.

"Mind you," she continued, trying to patch up her mistake, "you won't find a single bird inside the valley, and come to think about it, I never saw a bird's nest in all the time I've lived there. That's all really."

"I see," Gaspar said with a groan, giving Rosa a sidelong glare so intense that it sent a shiver through her body.

"I don't like to be glared at in that way, grasshopper," she hissed. "What's on your mind? Be straight with me. I don't have to accept help from any odd creature who comes along. So don't overstretch yourself to impress me with stories about your connections and the power you have over them. Who do you think you are? You're only a grasshopper, for pity's sake."

The grasshopper felt his anger welling up inside him, and had to struggle to hold it down. "As I said, Ladybird Rosa," he said in a sour voice, "there's a lot of thinking and planning to be done before I meet with my friends and put my thoughts across to them. I don't want to brag but I can almost guarantee they'll accept my proposal, as it'll be to their advantage as well. I can even go as far as say that Blossom Valley could easily be taken over, the spider got rid of, and then, my dear lady, the prince, the princess and the rest of them will be left totally unprotected and at anyone's mercy. So be a good girl and keep our conversation to yourself for if as much as a whisper gets out, I lose nothing while you, you'll see your chance for revenge crumble to nothing. Have I made myself, clear? I may have news in a few days, so stick around and I'll make sure to find you."

Without further word, the grasshopper turned his back on her and motioned to his gang to follow.

"Where are we heading to, boss?" one of his men asked. "Cause there's a few things we want to have out with you and there's no better time than now that they're fresh in our heads."

Gaspar flung both hands up. "Not now, not now, fellas. My head is spinning. I need a bit of time to sort my mind out. There will be plenty of time to talk after I've paid a visit to Blossom Valley and seen the spider."

The gang gasped. "You're crazy, boss," they said.

"I know what I'm doing, fellas," Gaspar said. "I need to see things for myself. You can't trust anyone these days. I'll meet you before sundown in the reeds on the west bank of Penny Creek."

Fifteen

Blossom Valley was fervently preparing for the celebration, as any day now the cuckoo would be flying over with his spring message.

The stage where the dancing, singing and acting would be performed was finished. But the repairs on the stands had fallen behind as senior rabbit carpenters were in hospital with injuries and broken legs.

Luckily, the jack rabbits, craftsmen in carpentry, offered a helping hand and in no time the stands were restored. Soon afterwards a buzz of activity took over as everyone did their bit to get Blossom Valley spick and span for the big day.

The hedgehogs were rolling along the stage and the stands, their spikes working hard on the wooden planks until they came out smooth and shiny.

The girl ants were making daisy chains, one for every creature to wear round their neck and some spares for visitors who might drop in.

Teams of squirrels and rabbits, trundling the wooden wheelbarrows uphill and downhill, chattering away, whistling and singing, were clearing paths, grass and flower beds of dead leaves, twigs and flower petals. They stored the twigs on the far northern hill, for as they did every spring, the herons would be picking those twigs up for their nest building.

Conti, a gourd swinging from each hand, tore to and fro to fetch water from the pond to water the plants that were wilting under the hot sun. The gourds were the large hollow fruit of a trailing plant that grew wild inside the valley. When their hard skin dried, the squirrels would chisel them into pails. Gourds were scattered across the grounds to provide water for the creatures, or a bath for the smaller birds, and it was Conti's responsibility to keep them full at all times.

The butterflies and bumblebees were making streamers with flowers of different, dazzling colours to decorate the stage and stands.

The crows promised they'd fly over places where funfairs were held and salvage those balloons that broke free from children's grasps.

Thelma was on her way to the hospital to cheer the sick and injured with the news that they'd soon be out to celebrate the arrival of spring. She was shielding her eyes from the harsh sunlight when she jolted to a halt. Her eyes widened in disbelief as she stared at the intruder. "What on earth are you doing, here?" she yelled. "This is private land and you're trespassing. Leave at once."

The grasshopper stooped, snapped the stem of a white daisy and waved it in the air. "I've come in peace. There's no need to be annoyed," he said, looking around. The sky was empty of birds but on the ground, a number of red squirrels had darted onto the bushes around him, all eyes fixed on him.

"I'm Gaspar," the grasshopper said with a grin, "head of a powerful and respectable family of grasshoppers. But before I state the reason for my visit, I need to put something straight and make it clear to you that I have as much right to be on this land as you have, cause the land belongs to us all and neither you nor any other creature, whether big or small, weak or powerful, can claim it as theirs. So I am not trespassing."

Holding her head right up, Thelma replied to his remark with defiance and pride in her voice. "This land, which the trees and ivy seclude from the outside world, has belonged to our ancestors for centuries and has been passed down to our generations. I should know better than you, grasshopper. So yes, this land is ours."

Gaspar was taken aback by Thelma's grand manner but only for a short second. He'd stashed some wicked lies in his head, certain that one of them would shackle the old spider's arrogance.

"That's a great shame, lady," he said with a devious grin, "cause my friends, the wood flies, are looking for a place to move in and Blossom Valley seems like a…"

"Stop!" Thelma cried out. "I want to hear nothing from you, for as far as time goes back, your kind, have been liars, bullies and deceivers."

Gaspar took a step closer to Thelma. His bloodshot eyes stared directly at hers and his hot breath almost touched her face. Thelma drew back in disgust.

"You've spoken badly of us, lady," he said angrily, "and you, being as clever as you make out, should know that all creatures are different and none of us are perfect, but we're not the names you've just called us. You have insulted the grasshoppers' world, and neither me nor my people will take kindly to it."

Thelma ignored his angry talk and said scornfully, "So, grasshopper, the wood flies have sent you to speak on their behalf, have they? If the wood flies want to move in with us," she went on, "they should state their wish themselves, not through a representative such as a grasshopper. We've never refused kindly creatures, and there's plenty of room in Blossom Valley." She wasn't keen on the wood flies living on their land but the grasshopper needn't know that. "You can tell the wood flies, they'll be welcomed here, only they'll have to come and see me."

Gaspar's temper was heating up and sweat started rolling down his craggy cheeks. But a cooling smile lit up his face as in that instant the spark in his brain ignited an explosive lie that would blast the spider. He swiped his arm across his runny nose and, picking his words carefully said. "The truth is, lady, the wood flies aren't bothered much about your land. It's your butterflies they want. The young leader, head of the wood fly swarms, heard about your butterflies and sneaked in to see them. He was enchanted by them, but his eyes settled on one with exceptional beauty, the one you call princess, I believe. He fell in love with her at first sight and wants to marry her. Don't worry about the rest – there are quite a few second-in-command grooms."

"Over my dead body will our princess or any of our butterflies marry a wood fly. Did you hear me, grasshopper? Now get out of here."

Grinding their chiselling teeth, the red squirrels shot out of the bushes and surrounded him.

"No need to use force, fellas," said the grasshopper, waving the white daisy in front of their eyes. "I'm almost done. There's one more thing, Thelma. Your name has been on the tip of my tongue all this time and it's just come to me. It is Thelma, isn't it? The wood flies are ferocious, brutal and stubborn. They always get what they've set their mind upon. They'll storm your valley and snatch your butterflies in front of your very eyes." With a horrible cackle the grasshopper turned his back and stalked away with the red squirrels at his heels.

George, who'd been within the valley, still recovering, found Thelma shaking. "We heard it all, Thelma," he said in a whisper. "Plato was with me and he has already alerted his scout bird to keep a close watch on the grasshopper and the wood flies. Don't be upset. We won't let any creature come into the valley. Anyway, the wood flies may not even exist."

"They do exist, George. There's a big population of them at Penny Clearing. It's not them that worry me, it's Rosa. This was her work, I know it was. The grasshopper knew all about us. He even knew my name. It's her that scares me George. She won't rest until the butterflies are…" she choked.

Sixteen

After he'd left Blossom Valley well behind, Gaspar sat in the shade of a tree and went over what had just taken place. He was chuffed that his lies had shaken the old spider. This was what he'd done his whole life. Posing as a powerful and respectable leader, he'd deceived, caused misery and ruined creatures' lives. But he was now tired of being on the run, hunted by those he'd wronged. This wood fly – Blossom Valley scheme of his, could be the biggest and most successful one yet and he'd be a fool to let it slip through his fingers. He could live in the luxury he'd dreamed about his whole miserable life. Thousands of hard working ants would provide the best grain in the region. He'd bring in families of grasshoppers from neighbouring and faraway places and gather a strong army of them. He'd make a family of his own, have sons, like any normal creature, and he would build the biggest and most powerful grasshopper dynasty to rule across Blossom Valley in the years to come. The wood flies would be his neighbours and trusted allies, and with their huge swarms, and his powerful army of grasshoppers no bird or other predator would attempt to threaten them.

With these tempting thoughts in his head and a huge smile across his face, Gaspar hopped towards Penny Reeds to meet his men.

It was Dafty who came out of the reeds to greet him. He was the youngest in the gang, nicknamed Dafty, because he was very naive. "How was Blossom Valley, boss?" he asked.

"It was good, Dafty," Gaspar replied flatly.

"I say, boss, did you mean what you said to the ladybird about helping her? What's in it for us, boss?" Dafty persisted.

"Ants, Dafty," Gaspar replied peevishly. "There're lots of ants in Blossom Valley, and what do ants, do? From dawn to dusk they collect all sorts of food, mainly grain, and stow it in their underground chambers. Well, they won't be doing much stowing away cause they'll be handing it over to us."

"But, boss…"

"I'm going to boss you good and proper if you don't stop firing stupid questions at me like that. You're doing my head in."

"Hold it there, boss," an old member of the gang interrupted. "The lad only wants to know, we all want to know. All along we've followed you through thick and thin and, with respect boss, you've led us into big trouble most of the time. You promised us we'd get something good out of each scheme of yours but it always went wrong and we ended up in nasty situations, fights and stuff. I lost one eye. Others lost limbs and some their lives. We've had enough, boss. We're tired of this life, I'm telling you."

Gaspar sat on the grass and motioned to the gang to do the same. He drew breath and began. "You're right to feel this way, fellas. I feel the same. We've had a hard life, I admit, but all this is about to change. I've been looking for a permanent and secure place for us all to settle down to a peaceful life and I believe Blossom Valley will do us nicely. That's why I went there to survey the place and I'm telling you, you're going to love it there. Besides, we won't have to worry about food. The ants will provide us with as much grain as we want. I have something big up my sleeve that will change our lives for good. Cheer up, fellas, a bright future awaits us. All that remains now is to get myself down to Penny Clearing and talk to the wood flies."

"The wood flies? Why, boss?" one of his men asked.

"To, offer them the opportunity to move into Blossom Valley with us. It's good to share the land with creatures that you know, and who better than the trustworthy wood flies whom we've known for donkeys' years?"

"Boss," Dug, the one eyed grasshopper, said, "are we going to be involved in fighting? If not, how are we going to get in Blossom Valley?"

"The wood flies, will do the fighting. Their swarms are huge and well trained to scare the life out of birds of any size. I'll contribute the plans that take brains to lay out. I have a very important task to deal with, fellas, and must leave you now. I will bring you news tomorrow."

He walked out of the reeds, heading for Penny Hollow, a secluded safe place where in peace and quiet he would go over the scheme he would put across to the wood flies, the next morning.

Seventeen

Nothing much had changed since the last time Gaspar had been down this way. The majestic old oak tree still stood there, its great limbs gnarled and darkened, stretching across the clearing. He shaded his eyes from the dazzling sun and slowly trudged along.

The old oak tree hollow was crammed with wood flies. A huge number were chasing each other up and down the enormous oak tree trunk and loads more were loafing on the grass. The humming was loud and the smell unwelcoming.

One wood fly spotted him and sluggishly walked towards him. It was his old mate, Wilfred, head of the wood flies. His face was withered with age and his swollen belly wobbled like soft jelly as he moved closer.

"Well, well, if it isn't Gaspar, our long lost mate," he said with a chuckle. "Come and see fellas."

Heaps of wood flies poured out of the hollow as if tipped out of a huge bucket. They blinked and peered at him, as if they'd just woken up or had sore eyes.

"We had you for dead mate," Wilfred said, "cause you do get yourself mixed up in some dodgy doings and…"

"I'm done with dodgy stuff," Gaspar interrupted. "And if you're asking about my gang, they're still loyal to me. I left them behind cause it's something very important I've come to talk to you about. But first let me hear your news, Wilfred. How has it been for you?"

"We aren't complaining, mate," Wilfred replied, patting his belly. "Life's been good for us. Food is plentiful around here and our women look after us well. Other than that, it's the same old life. Mind you, we're glad now that spring's here. We can stretch out in the sun, the best part of the day."

"Some life," Gaspar snorted. "Dull, boring no excitement no purpose. Idle life has made you obese, Wilfred. You need to be active, have fun, exercise."

"We do exercise," a group of wood flies resting on the brim of the hollow blurted out.

"We go over the fields." Wilfred took over. "We do our formation flights. We're the best in the wood fly world, you know. Mind you, me and my age group don't do much. We mostly watch and advise." Then he went silent, staring at the grasshopper, his eyes full of suspicion. "What is it you're after, Gaspar? You haven't showed up to give us advice on healthy living, that's for sure. So I'd better warn you, if it's anything to do with your old pranks, you're wasting your time and ours."

"I know that a lot of my doings haven't been good, Wilfred, and some have been terrible." Gaspar tried to sound regretful. "But it takes all sorts to make the world, doesn't it? Those bad old days are long gone. Age has changed me to a better being. No more scheming, bullying and fighting. I've done it all. I've been looking for a place for me and my men to settle down and lead a peaceful life and that's the reason I'm here, Wilfred. Wandering through the meadow the other day, I overheard some ladybirds talking about a place called Blossom Valley. Have you heard of it?"

Wilfred let his head drop in a nod, then opened his mouth and let out a long loud yawn. "I'm getting bored, mate," he moaned. "Where are you taking us with all this?"

"Be patient, it'll get more interesting as I go on. The ladybirds were saying that Blossom Valley is a magical place where butterfly princes and princesses live, and I couldn't believe my ears when they said an enormous spider runs the place. To cut a long story short, I found the place and sneaked in. Mates, you've never seen anything like it. Its beauty blew me away. I was trotting along, trying to take it all in, when the spider stomped in front of me. *This place is private land and you are trespassing*, she said. *I am the head of this place and I order you out or I'll have you removed.* Five or six squirrels darted out of nowhere and stood in front of me waiting for the spider's order to tear me apart. I was scared stiff, of course I was, but I was determined to stand up to her. *This isn't private land*, I said to her. *It belongs to us all to live in, and no creature whether small or big, weak or mighty, can claim it as theirs.* Isn't that right, mate? Correct me if you think I'm wrong."

"No, you're not wrong, mate," Wilfred replied, shaking his head.

"No, no," the wood flies mumbled together, shaking their heads.

"Once we had a fox," an old wood fly started. "Do you remember, fellas?"

They all nodded.

"A pack of hounds were after her. She dashed into our hollow. We didn't turn her away cause it was our own home. Instead we blocked the hollow with our bodies. The hounds lost her scent and we were chuffed we'd saved her life. Isn't that right, fellas?"

"Y…eees" they all groaned.

"Private land, be blowed," said the old wood fly, belching loudly. "Farmers call their land private, cause they're humans and buy the farmland from other humans, if you know what I mean."

"Well said, my friend," said Gaspar, eager to carry on. "Going back to the spider, I said to her, *me and my friends the wood flies are looking for a place to live and Blossom*

Valley seems nice enough. So what makes you think you've got the right to refuse us? Without any hesitation and with an air of superiority she said, *I have complete authority over this place and wood flies are not the sort of creatures I'd welcome in. They're rough and foul and I wouldn't welcome conniving grasshoppers either. You've heard my answer,* she said, *now get out.* I was boiling with anger and wanted to give her a kick when the squirrels darted at me, gnashing their teeth." Gaspar drew breath and was about to carry on, when Wilfred stopped him.

"Hold it there, mate," he said, cause you've got me a little confused. Did you ever hear us say we're in need of a home? It's you and your gang that have always been homeless. Besides, who gave you the right to speak to the spider on our behalf? Cause I'm telling you her remarks have upset me real deep." He gave Gaspar a long considering look. "If I know you, and I know you well, you've never given a toss about us nor, anyone else. All you've ever cared was what you'd get out of it. So what's the catch, grasshopper? What's inside that cunning brain of yours?"

Never before had Wilfred called him grasshopper, and that worried Gaspar. Beads of sweat broke out on his forehead and his jaw twitched nervously. He glanced over at the crowds of wood flies and his gaze rested on Wilfred's suspicious face.

"There's no catch mate," he said with certainty in his voice. "It's genuine through and through. I have friends, of course I have, who'd give their right arm to live in place like Blossom Valley. But they're the troublesome lot from my old days and I've broken away from them. Blossom Valley is a vast place, too big for a handful of us. My gang has shrunk since I last saw you." He faked sadness in his voice. "I've lost some of my best men. You've been my mates for donkeys' years and

I trust you cause you're honest creatures. This is the reason I'm here today, to offer you this golden opportunity to move with me and my men to Blossom Valley.

"Your population has grown since I last saw you, and the squalid conditions you live in crammed up in these hollows are unacceptable for you but more so for your females and the young ones. Blossom Valley is a paradise with gardens you've never imagined, streams and ponds where you can wash yourselves or have a swim and there's more trees and hollows than you can count. The females will love it there, especially the young ones who can mix with the noble butterflies, and you never know, some butterfly prince may fall in love with them."

The young female wood flies hid themselves behind each other and squealed bashfully.

Gaspar spotted the excitement in their eyes, and the shy smile that came to their faces and a tingle of encouragement went through him. "Well?" he prompted Wilfred with a long stare.

But the old wood fly, wise to the grasshopper's devious nature, remained unimpressed and disinterested.

The grasshopper coughed to draw everyone's attention for all he could do now was bluff.

"Well mates," he said trying to hide all trace of disappointment, "you've heard all that I said. If you're still, doubting me you've only got to say so, and I'll be on my way."

Wilfred glanced at his people and his people glanced at him. It seemed that Gaspar's words had brightened their cheerless faces and put a sparkle in their dull eyes.

"I must say, Gaspar," he began, "you did well to stand up to the spider the way you did. Her arrogance has angered me but her harsh words against us wood flies have hurt me deeply cause all us creatures are what we are. That's how nature made us; we didn't choose what to be. But we all have a purpose on this earth and no creature more privileged than us should despise us. So somebody should tell the spider that. As to whether we want to move, it's not up to me to decide. I've handed the leadership over to my eldest son, Hugo, who makes the decisions now."

"How come you have retired, Wilfred? Have you been in poor health?" Gaspar asked his question in a deep tone of concern to hide his disappointment. A young new leader might not fall for his scheme. It was possible he'd heard Wilfred talk about Gaspar's devious past, and would be wary of him. Shame, for it had been going so well.

"No mate," Wilfred replied, "I'm as fit as a fiddle. Hugo is a good son, but I still guide him and I'm certain he will be a sensible and fair leader to our people."

Eighteen

Gaspar was about to carry on, when two young wood flies pushed their way through the crowd and came running in, crying and gasping for breath.

"What is it, children?" Wilfred looked concerned. "Get your breath back and then tell me."

"Hugo was cruel to our fathers," one of them cried between sobs. "They were having a spat, a disagreement really, when Hugo rushed at them and threw them in a deep muddy puddle. They nearly drowned. When they were able to stand on their feet, he ordered one of his men to lock them up in the detention hollow. Why? They did no wrong. It is very unfair," both children cried and ran out.

Heads shook with disapproval, and muffled whisperings spread across the crowds of wood flies but died down sharply. Dead silence followed and all heads turned as one towards the voices that were approaching. The crowds shifted back as a young wood fly who carried himself in a dignified way and some three others who trailed behind him walked in.

"The children were upset, Hugo," Wilfred said in a deep grave voice. "You were cruel to their fathers. Is that so?"

"I wasn't cruel. I split them up before they came to blows. They slipped in the mud. I sent them to the detention hollow because we need to set examples for our children," Hugo retorted.

Wilfred shook his head. He didn't look happy. He shuffled his body into a more comfortable position and turned to

Gaspar. "This is Hugo, my eldest son," he said. "The other three are my younger ones."

Hugo walked slowly and stood in the middle of the crowd. He was tall, lean and handsome. His sharp and intelligent eyes turned from his people and came to rest on the grasshopper.

"Me and your father go back a long time," Gaspar said, beaming at him. "Pleased, to meet you Hugo. I was speaking to your..."

"No need to repeat yourself, grasshopper," Hugo said, cutting him off bluntly. "Me and my brothers were very close and heard it all to the end." Then Hugo, arms behind his back took a few paces forward to face Gaspar and for a long second his eyes held him in a curious searching stare.

"That's it, I was right," Gaspar thought to himself. "This smug young wood fly will ruin my plan or worse, kick me out." But to his great relief, Hugo looked away and in a formal voice, he said. "Now, grasshopper, tell us why you're here. Are you seeking revenge on the spider, or you're aiming at something else?"

Gaspar drew air through his nose to stop it running, and with an air of confidence he said, "I'll gain nothing by seeking revenge, though I feel bitter cause her cruel remarks about the grasshopper world and the wood fly population were totally unfair. Like your father, I strongly believe somebody should tell the spider that. As to what I'm aiming at, it's nothing big, just a small corner in the beautiful land of Blossom Valley where me and my men can live a peaceful life with the wood fly population as our good neighbours. But In a scornful manner the spider has made it clear she won't allow wood flies or grasshoppers on her private land. So there's no other way but to move in by force."

Wilfred shuddered. "You mean go to war with the creatures of Blossom Valley?"

"You're putting words in my mouth, mate," Gaspar protested. "I never said war, cause that's an ugly word. You go to war when there's an enemy to wipe out. There's no enemy in Blossom Valley, only a handful of creatures. I went there on a scouting mission, didn't I? I said by force, cause that's the only way to get what you want. Humans do it all the time."

"We're not humans," Wilfred argued. "We're wood flies, and a peaceful sort, I'll have you know. Violence doesn't solve problems. It brings disaster, suffering and pain."

"Father, listen to me. If we chose to settle in a place where rabbits, hares and moles burrowed, bees, wasps and birds nested, would any of those creatures turn us away? Did the birds of Blossom Valley ask permission to nest there? Did the squirrels, hares, rabbits, the ants and any sort of bugs, ask the spider's permission to walk, hop or crawl on the land of Blossom Valley? I'm certain they didn't. So why can't we do the same?"

"Cause," Gaspar blurted in, "the spider doesn't want the wood flies or the grasshoppers on her land."

Hugo's eyes flashed with anger. He stood bold upright and raised his voice to be heard across the clearing and beyond. "Discriminating between creatures is cruel and should not happen in a free world. I believe it's time we brought pride to the wood fly world and told the spider we're equal to any of them and don't deserve her hostility and contempt."

"Slow down, slow down son," Wilfred shouted. "You're young and overwhelmed with pride and ambition. We're not seeking revenge here. We never have. Revenge leads to conflict, to death, to distraction and misery. Besides, there're our people to think of, our women, the young ones and the elderly. The safety of our people comes first and you'll do well to remember that, Hugo."

"I am young yes, and I am ambitious, but I am not foolish. I will not be seeking revenge, father, I'll be claiming my people's rights."

Wilfred struggled to stand on his feet and shouted. "Enough! Proper decisions can't be made when the soul isn't calm or the mind clear. We'll continue tomorrow when tempers have soothed. I have half a mind to go to Blossom Valley myself and talk to the spider. Have a peaceful argument."

"Never," Hugo shouted. "Where is your pride, father? We are not going to plead with the spider to take us in. This is a new world we live in now, father, not the good all days you and your cronies have known."

"I can go," Gaspar offered eagerly. "I'll have no problem pleading with her. In fact it would be better if I did, cause I've already seen and spoken to her."

"No, grasshopper," Hugo said sharply. "We don't need a representative."

Gaspar was hurt but tried hard not to show it.

"I haven't been beaten yet," he thought. "My scheme hasn't totally collapsed. It has roused this stubborn young leader. It has driven him to rage. Rage leads to revenge and revenge will lead Hugo to Blossom Valley. All is not lost."

"Before I bid you good day," Gaspar said with a tone of flattery in his voice, "I want you to know that I admire you, Hugo. You are what a great leader should be. Whatever decision you make, bear in mind that me and my men will be glad to support you."

"I don't need your flattery, grasshopper, and neither do I need your support," Hugo said sharply. "A handful of untrained grasshoppers would present problems instead of offering support. But thanks," Hugo concluded and walked away.

Neither Gaspar nor the wood flies were aware that all this time Swift, the scout bird, had been hiding in the old oak tree and was about to fly to Blossom Valley to report all that had taken place. But when he spotted Gaspar in conversation with Rosa a few yards away from the old oak tree he carefully flew down, hid inside a cluster of thick grass, and listened to all that went on.

***

"What the hell are you doing here? Have you been following me?" Gaspar was fuming. "I told you I'd come and find you if I had news. Actually I was on my way to do just that."

"Were you now?" Rosa said, laughing sarcastically. "Then I saved you the journey. I came out to look for you and, lo and behold, where do I find you? So the wood flies are the powerful friends you talked to me about, are they?"

Fury welled up inside Gaspar. He leapt at her and grabbed her neck. "You've been spying on me Rosa," he growled and tightened his grip. "I won't have that. I told you to be a good girl and wait. Why have you been spying on me? Tell me or I'll throttle you."

"Try and I'll scream my head off. The wood flies will pour out and I'll tell them who you really are. Look, look, they're coming."

As Gaspar turned round to look, his grip on Rosa loosened and she got away. She heard Gaspar say in a rasping voice, "I'll get you Rosa, I swear l will."

Rosa waited until all was quiet, and cautiously crawled towards the old oak tree. She hadn't gone far, when she bumped into a large number of wood flies feeding on some decayed plant roots. "Which one of you is Hugo?" she asked in a husky whisper.

"Who wants to know?" Hugo asked, shooting Rosa a

frosty look.

"I'm Rosa, and I've come to warn you not to trust the grasshopper. He is a scheming, conniving creature and everything he has told you is a lie. I've lived in Blossom Valley for a very long time and I know how things work there. I can help you get inside the valley without conflict and loss of life. I know of a good and tested way but I can only reveal it to the leader."

Rosa moved slowly away and Hugo followed her into the thick foliage of the elder tree, and listened to what she had to say.

When Hugo went back to his feeding and Rosa flew away, Swift sped off for Blossom Valley.

***

Gaspar was restless. A niggling feeling was telling him that Rosa was up to something, and he needed to find out what it was. He took Dug, the one eyed grasshopper, and another two and went out searching for her. Gaspar's instinct told him to try Penny Clearing first. His instinct proved to be right. Rosa was there. Her head stuck out from the grass blades, quite close to the old oak tree.

"Hello, my lovely," Gaspar said with a beastly grin on his face. "Fancy finding you here! Were you planning to visit the wood flies?"

"No I wasn't," Rosa replied. "I went on a long flight and I was having a rest. Is that a crime?"

"Too many lies, Rosa, too many lies," Gaspar grunted. "But they're ending here. Put her in the wire cage, fellas, and bolt it securely. Leave the cage on the banks of Penny River. Soon the water will carry her downstream and out into the ocean."

"Gaspar, don't do this to me. I'm begging you. I promise I'll do as you tell me. Please!" Rosa cried.

The grasshopper turned his back and leapt away.

Rosa started screaming, crying and banging her head against the cage walls. "He promised me a life of luxury in Blossom Valley and look at me now! Caged like a rat in a trap. Be warned! He'll do the same to you. He'll get rid of you, mark my words. What has he given you all the years you've been serving him, doing the dirty work for him? Nothing but misery, look at you! Don't you think you deserve better? This new scheme of his will fail, I'm sure it will. He'll be hurt and he'll turn nasty towards you. Get rid of him and start a new life as far away from him as possible."

"She's right," Dug whispered to the other two. "We must put an end to this miserable life of ours, be free of him, go where we want and do as we please. We can stick together or go our separate ways. Let her out, fellas, bring the cage here. The boss is bound to come and see that the job has been done. When I raise my right arm to scratch my brow, we'll surround him, get hold of him and force him in the cage. No second thoughts, no sentiments. Agreed?"

"Hello, fellas," Gaspar called in a crisp, chirpy voice. "Job's done?"

"We've always obeyed your orders boss, haven't we?" Dug replied, and raised his right arm.

All three grabbed Gaspar and pushed him into the cage.

"What's your game, fellas? Surely this is a joke. You're having a laugh, aren't you? Now let me out."

"We should have done this a long time ago," said Dug. "We'd still be your slaves if it weren't for that ladybird."

"What? You set her free?" Gaspar growled.

"Yes, boss," said Dug. "She's free and at long last we'll be free too! Free from you and your schemes!" He held the cage tightly in his hand and hurled it into the river. The swift current carried the cage downstream and out of sight.

Nineteen

Plato had been in Penny Wood a few minutes and was looking forward to a peaceful nap on his tree top when he picked up the message from Swift summoning him to Blossom Valley and gathered that Swift must be bringing news from the wood flies. He ruffled his feathers, flapped his wings and took off. Thelma and George were waiting for him.

Before long Swift joined them, briefly nodded his head in greeting, and without much ado started to report all he had heard up in the old oak tree.

After Swift had finished, Plato, who'd been listening carefully, spoke in a plain voice. "It is clear the wood flies were angered by the grasshopper's lie that Blossom Valley refuses to allow foul creatures such as them on their land. I believe the wood flies, could live with this, for they are not an easily offended sort of creatures nor are they vindictive enough to mount an invasion of Blossom Valley. But along comes Hugo, the young wood fly leader who gripped by enthusiasm and pride, visualises himself as a great military figure leading his men against Blossom Valley. He sees himself and his people settled in the magical gardens – as the grasshopper described them–and he, a celebrated hero flying amongst the graceful butterflies. To keep his dream alive he has to act fast, for fear the enthusiasm of his people might wear off, or us be alerted."

Thelma jumped to her feet. "We must start preparing Blossom Valley for an imminent invasion, for this young

Hugo is driven by passion and madness to get what he wants and could cause us unimaginable pain. The wood flies must, I repeat, *must* be prevented from getting inside the Valley."

"Thelma is right," Plato said to George. "We have no time to lose. I want you to be by my side at all times. Being a night bird, my vision is weak in the day, so you will be my second in command, as they say in the military world." Then, turning to Swift, he said.

"Good work, Swift! Thank you. Before you're off, find the blackbird, sparrow and crow flock leaders and tell them I'll be meeting them on Thistle Hill by the black rock before sundown. If they want to know the reason, you're free to tell them.

"I'll do that, Plato," said Swift, "but before I go, there're things that took place outside Penny Clearing you need to hear." He told them in detail about the brawl between Gaspar and Rosa, and her meeting with Hugo.

"Yesterday, quite by chance," Swift carried on, "I spotted three grasshoppers pushing Rosa into a wire cage and Gaspar watching from close by. When Gaspar had left, Rosa managed to turn the three grasshoppers against their boss by saying, amongst other things, that his scheme with the wood flies would fail and their life would be as miserable as before. They believed her and set her free. Her words must have fuelled their anger and ignited some spark of freedom inside them, for when Gaspar came to check that the job had been done, they locked him in the cage and threw it in the river. I thought you needed to know," he said then disappeared into the clouds.

"I'm glad the grasshopper is out of the way, but Rosa is alive," Thelma said with a sigh.

"Hugo must have laughed at Rosa's sleeping weed plan, Thelma," Plato said with some amusement in his voice. "He wants invasion and conflict, to show off his leadership and heroism. Hugo is itching for glory. His egoism would never allow a meagre ladybird to win his battle and anyway, they'd be needing tons of sleeping weed to put our birds and the entire valley to sleep, and they couldn't get tons out of the small sleeping weed Rosa knows of. Now, Thelma, put Rosa out of your mind and turn your thoughts away from your fears. Put on a brave face and talk to the creatures inside the valley. Remember, creatures can pick up on your anxiety. Tell Tawny Owl to have her team on standby. The first aid tent must be sited by the gate. She'll know the rest and, Thelma, it is going to be alright, trust me."

Conti was the first to be told. "Oh my! Oh my! The wood flies are coming!" He burst into a wild croak and began diving in and out of the water like a demented frog.

"Stop it, Conti!" Thelma shouted. "There's no need to be alarmed."

"I'm not alarmed," Conti spluttered, "I'm excited. Oh my! Oh my!"

The rest of the creatures were neither excited nor afraid. Only Speedo had something to say. "I'll be alright myself cause I'll scoot into my shell and stay there, but what's going to happen to the ants, Thelma?"

"You don't have to worry about them, Speedo. They'll be safe in their underground chambers. Everything will be okay."

***

Meanwhile, the bird leaders flew to Thistle Hill to find Plato waiting for them.

"Gentlemen," he said with a solemn expression on his face, "I trust Swift has told you about the disturbing situation we might have to face. I presume you'll want to refresh on air defence…"

"No need for that, Owl," the blackbird leader replied with a touchy note in his voice. "We are well trained and always prepared to face a sky enemy, and that, as you may know, can happen quite often across the skies."

"I didn't mean you might lack skill. Please don't take offence," Plato said timidly.

"Being a night bird, I miss most activities that take place across the skies during the day."

"You provide the brains, Owl. We will do the work. We're here to listen to your plan," said the sparrow leader, who had always been a bird of few words.

"As you wish, gentlemen," said Plato. "You take your normal flight path to the fields. Before you reach the old oak tree, you dip a good deal. The wood flies will have their eyes pinned to the sky. They'll see you and believe we're unaware of their plans and the valley is left empty of birds. Before you get to the fields take a wide turn to the right, fly over Penny Marshes, straight into Blossom Valley and spread out on the elm trees. The crows will split into four units and camp on the north, south, east and western walls. Swift will tell us exactly when, which could be as early as tomorrow. Before I tell you the plan and the signal you'll be responding to, I wish to stress this. The enemy – I hate to use this word – are the frivolous wood flies who have fallen for the grasshopper's scam. So I urge you to show a little mercy."

The blackbird leader spoke. "We appreciate your words, Plato. They're good and wise but when there's a fight or attack, or whatever you want to call it, it's usually the weak and innocent that end up dead. The wood flies, though frivolous as you called them, are not weak, but ferocious, barbaric and very dangerous, for they attack in volume. Our loyalty, you'll agree, lies with our flocks and I'm certain the other leaders will agree as well."

"Fair enough, gentlemen," said Plato. "I can't argue with that. "Now, come in closer for the next bit of the plan is crucial and it must be said in a whisper."

The bird leaders crowded close to Plato and with great attention listened to the plan he delivered.

Twenty

Sometime later that day, Hugo returned to face the crowds of wood flies that spread out by the old oak tree.

"Where is father?" Hector whispered close to Hugo's ear.

"He's resting in the old men's hollow. He's been hindering my plans. He's old and stubborn and lives in an age gone by. Things are different now. We have to move with the times, Hector. Anyway, he'll be better off there. His cronies will keep him good company."

Hugo walked a few paces closer to the crowds and his voice thundered out. "My people, tomorrow when the sun shows its full face over Sunrise Hill our swarms, led by my brother Hector, my second in command, and me, will attempt a surprise landing on Blossom Valley."

An old female wood fly suddenly sprang up and blurted out. "You're leading our men to this surprise landing as you call it, but for all we know it could turn into war. We don't want to lose our sons, brothers and husbands for the sake of exchanging the ordinary life we've lived happily, for the snobbish upper-crust Blossom Valley. Who wants a change anyway?"

"We do! We do!" the younger wood fly generations cried out.

Hugo raised his hand, gesturing for silence. "There will be no war," he said with calm confidence in his voice. "The surprise landing will be a kind of protest of right against wrong. Our right to live on the land the spider selfishly claims as hers, her wrongfulness in denying us this right and insulting us with her mean, hurtful remarks."

Then Hugo's voice brimming with pride rose across Penny Clearing. "We mustn't let the privileged walk over the ordinary. The spider needs to learn that the wood flies are as important as any of her creatures and we have a right to invade anywhere, if it means a better life for our people."

"Yeeess! Yeeess!" yelled the wood flies, thrusting their fists above their heads.

Exhausted by the burst of enthusiasm, pride and emotion, Hugo paused for breath. Then addressing the old female by her name he spoke again. "I respect your opinion, Anthea, as I do the opinion of all our people. But I believe a change will bring a renewed existence to our community, better conditions, and a better life. So I urge those of you who have second thoughts to raise their hands now."

One single hand rose, that of Anthea's.

"That's it then," said Hugo as he glared at Anthea, "a unanimous decision. Now I want all the females, children and elderly to move to where our brothers Phillip, Darius and Phelan are standing. They, together with our father, will take care of things. All men fall in line six abreast, march in the middle of the clearing and wait for orders."

As everyone started to move, Anthea blurted out. "We were happier with Wilfred, our old faithful, fair and caring leader. Where is he by the way, Hugo?"

Hugo grabbed the arm of one of his men and whispered in his ear. "When everyone has gone from here, take Anthea to the women's detention hollow. Make sure the bolt is secure."

Out in the clearing Hugo divided the men into two units. Hector leading his, would go out first. Hugo would keep well behind until Hector and his men were over the wall and inside the valley. "We'll be camping out here," said Hugo. "Try and get a good night's sleep, for a hard day awaits us tomorrow."

At the crack of dawn, the wood flies were lined up and, after a brief body exercising, they took a short flight over Penny Clearing, practised their formation manoeuvres, then camouflaged themselves in the undergrowth, their eyes pinned to the sky, waiting for the Blossom Valley birds to fly over the clearing and on to the fields.

"This is it, men," cried Hugo. "The sky is now empty of birds which means, the valley is left unprotected and free for the taking. Let's do it. Hector! Assemble your men. You are going out first as planned."

"Come on, men!" Hector ordered. "It's time we took flight. Keep your humming low or try not to hum at all. Sound travels fast in the wind."

Swift raced to Blossom Valley with a brief message. "Hector is about to set out. Hugo will follow."

***

Plato and George took their posts on the top branch of the big fir tree. The two birds sat side by side, silently watching and waiting. George broke the silence. "Aren't you at all anxious, Plato?" he asked in a quavering whisper.

Plato remained deaf to George's question. His eyes still and watchful, stared ahead without blinking. A second passed and George poked Plato with the tip of his left wing. "I can see a grey cloud in the horizon racing towards us. Can you see it?"

"Not clearly," answered Plato, "but I'm certain it isn't a storm cloud."

Seconds lingered before George poked him again. "Can't you see they're almost upon us, Plato?"

Unperturbed, Plato turned his eyes to George. "Have some faith in me, Crow. I know what I'm doing." At once, he brought both his wings over his beak and blew through the feathers.

110

As the signal went out, the blackbirds flew above the trees, flapping and soaring until the sky was painted black. They dived and rose, tipped and turned, gradually falling one by one into a stacking formation. A line of blackbirds hovered in mid-air, then another above them, and lastly a third line. It seemed they were attempting to create a barrier of some sort.

"Hector!" one wood fly screamed, "I can see birds! What's happening?"

"We've been set up, fellas!" Hector bellowed. "Keep your spirits up! Fight! In the name of the wood fly world, let's show them what we're made of."

Spurred on by Hector's cries, his unit, humming with fury charged forward.

The blackbirds stretched their wings out and the wood flies smashed onto a rigid impenetrable black wall. Huge numbers of shrieking wood flies dropped dead on the ground.

"Volume and belly!" blasted Hector, and at once his men reassembled into a solid mass of wood fly bodies and charged like bats out of hell crashing onto the blackbirds' bellies. The impact was tremendous. The black wall dissolved and the blackbirds, squawking with agonizing pain, fell on the ground. Some were injured, other died and the rest retreated to the nearest trees.

The wood flies raced for the ivy wall. Plato let out the crows' signal. The crows rushed out of the ivy, stretched their wings, and with sharp swatting blows, knocked the wood flies down by the dozen. Those rare few that escaped the crows' blows were bombarded with volleys of acorns and fir cones by the squirrels until every last one had fallen.

Meanwhile on the ground, trained teams of squirrels and rabbits with Red Cross bands on heads and arms and carrying stretchers, were picking up the injured birds and those wood flies that stirred. They rushed them to the Red Cross tent where Tawny Owl and her team could see to them.

Twenty One

Hugo knew they'd been set up, for he'd heard his brother's voice in the wind. His blood boiled with rage and his eyes blazed with a thirst for revenge.

"My men!" he rumbled, "in the name of our people, I urge you to show courage, wit and no mercy. We must get inside Blossom Valley, whatever it takes. Keep your spirit burning and let us gather speed for Blossom Valley."

"Plato!" George cried. "Are you blind? Hugo's unit is but a stone's throw away. Can't you hear the roaring?"

"You're shaking, George. Are you cold?" Plato turned and looked at him with a teasing twinkle in his eyes.

"Are all owls as unruffled, as you, Plato? My heart is about to pop out of my chest and you find time to joke?"

"Then compose yourself," he answered calmly. "I've got it under complete control." He cleared his throat and let out the sparrows' signal.

With a deafening rustle, the sparrows emerged from the trees, slowly falling into a V pattern. They zoomed high in the air and hovered until the wood flies were right underneath them. The sparrow leader gave the order. The V nosed down and crashed on Hugo's unit with such force, it sent masses of wood flies flying in the air then dropping on the ground like pellets in a hail storm.

Suddenly a young quavering voice filled with pain and terror cried. "Stop it! What are we fighting for? Our leaders lied to us. They have led us into death and distraction. I don't want to die. No one wants to die."

The sparrow leader told his birds to dissolve the pattern and retreat to the trees. He flew close to the stricken young wood fly. "You are right, young fellow," he said. "But in a conflict, there will always be losses. It is inevitable. Some of my birds lay dead on the ground. Your losses are greater. I'm sorry but it wasn't our choice. We had to defend our home. Retreat fellows. Go back to your families."

"Where is Hector? Where is Hugo to lead us out of here?" shouted the young voice.

"Hector is dead," an old wood fly's voice replied, "and Hugo has just fallen. Good riddance to him! I hope he breathes his last breath on this land. I shall lead you home. Follow me!"

Then it all stopped. The sky emptied and stillness fell.

***

Lying on the stretcher, Hugo tossed and turned, then kept still. One of his men raised his head and stared at him. "Are you dead?" he whispered.

"No, I'm not," Hugo replied. "Lie down and pretend you're dead. Pass on the word to those that stir. No questions. It's an order."

Two rabbits carrying the stretcher rushed to the tent and left it on the ground. "What do you want us to do with them, Tawny Owl?" they asked. "Some of them seemed alive when we picked them up but haven't moved a limb since. Shall we empty them into the basket with the dead?"

"No," she replied, "not before I make certain I can do nothing to save them. Leave them there and run off to pick up the rest."

No one would be watching a heap of dead wood flies on a stretcher, Hugo thought. So he and those few left alive crept out and, edging along the ivy wall, squeezed themselves into the valley.

"We need to find where the butterflies are kept," he said.

"Are you after the butterflies? Why? Do you fancy them, then?"

"You're being stupid now. Butterflies may be beautiful but they are vain and brainless. We have some very pretty females in our community. I can have any of them. Besides, it is best to keep to our own kind. I want to get my hands on the spider and she's sure to be somewhere close to the butterflies. The spider must be caught and taken alive to our people. I'll think what to do with the butterflies afterwards. I may have to kill them."

Hugo and his men crawled and wriggled across different parts of the valley for a long time, searching and listening for any sounds, when at last one of his men said in a hushed voice, "there, there. Look! I can see a spider pacing up and down. Is it her?"

"It must be her," whispered Hugo. "There's only one spider in Blossom Valley."

Taking great care and looking behind their backs, they crept through the thick grass until they were very close.

"Now," Hugo whispered and his men pounced on her from behind.

Thelma was stunned but her voice came out firm and commanding. "What do you think you're doing? Get off my back at once or…"

"Cut out that attitude of authority and importance, spider. It won't wash with me. I am Hugo, the wood fly leader. We will take you to Penny Clearing, where in front of my people you'll be punished for your selfishness and your cruel remarks against us. I will see, as leader of my population, that you're hanged from our old oak tree until your last breath leaves you and your body shrivels."

"I have done nothing wrong to be punished for," Thelma retorted. "I did not refuse to allow your people to move in with us, and never said a cruel word against the wood fly world. It was all the grasshopper's deceitful lies. And *you*, a mindless young leader who let a renowned cunning, scheming creature lead you on, it is *you* who should be held responsible. It is *you* who caused the loss of half your population, and in the end it might be *you* who will hang from your old oak tree."

Hugo was taken aback, shaken by Thelma's harsh, offensive speech, and it hurt worse, for deep down he knew there was truth in it.

"Shut up! Shut up!" he ordered, his eyes flashing with anger. He gestured to his men and they knocked her down. Some fell on top of her.

"Where are the butterflies, spider?" Hugo demanded.

"They've been taken away to safety," she answered. She wriggled and turned and kicked to free herself, but couldn't shake off the weight of so many wood flies on her back. In the struggle to keep her down the wood flies broke some of her legs and damaged some of her eyes.

"Where are the butterflies?" insisted Hugo.

Thelma gave an almighty push and managed to rid herself of the weight, and with great effort she stood on her remaining legs.

"The butterflies, like all of us in Blossom Valley, have done no wrong," she said, "and if you try as much as lay a finger on them, our birds will fall upon your people like a ton of bricks. The entire population down to the last wood fly will be wiped out and there will be no place for you to hide, for you'll be hunted down and hanged from your old oak tree." Her legs wouldn't support her any longer and she collapsed.

Deep inside the pen, Princess Estella kept trying to come out but Gloria and her girls blocked her way. In the end, determined to see what was happening out there, she pushed and barged and forced her way to the front of the pen. When she saw the wood flies carrying Thelma away, she let out a horrified scream. "No!"

Conti the frog who was at the hospital helping Tawny Owl's team, heard. At once he hopped outside and at the top of his voice croaked once, twice, and a third time.

Plato and George were still up on the fir tree, silent, staring at the empty horizon.

The sound sent a jolt through George. He nudged Plato. "Did you hear? The frog hasn't croaked like this before. Something is happening." He shot off his perch and Plato followed him to the butterflies' pen.

Princess Estella was crying her eyes out and couldn't utter a word. Gloria, though shaken, spoke to Plato. "We knew something was going on out there but we never imagined it could be wood flies so close to the pen. We couldn't risk going out. But Princess Estella managed to push her way to the entrance of the pen. She saw the wood flies taking Thelma away and she yelled. Then we heard the frog's alarming croak."

"It's going to be alright, Gloria," said Plato. "We are going to find Thelma and bring her back. Go and tell the butterflies."

George stayed outside the tent while Plato went in to speak to Tawny Owl. "You must be exhausted, Tawny Owl."

"I'm not complaining," she said. "My team and I did all that was possible. We attended to the wounded and the dying. Sadly, we suffered quite a few losses ourselves. Some few have recovered. The seriously wounded are in hospital where my team know what to do. I'll be going there shortly myself. The dead wood flies, a large number of them, we kept in the brown basket. The treated injured, are in the green. What are you planning to do with them?"

"The hares will take them in the ambulance cart to Penny Clearing. George and I will be flying there as well. The wood flies have taken Thelma. We're going to bring her home."

Twenty Two

The hares had unloaded the baskets when Plato and George got to Penny Clearing. Plato gestured to them and in the next instant the ambulance cart zoomed out of sight leaving clouds of dust behind.

Plato took a few steps forward and looked around. Something was wrong. Huge numbers of wood flies were walking away from Penny Clearing. Plato stopped a mother who was carrying two little children on her back, and asked her. "What's happened? Where are you going?"

"Penny Clearing isn't ours any longer," she said, her eyes filling with tears. "When our men were fighting in Blossom Valley, a swarm of ferocious horse flies marched in. We were mostly females, children and the elderly. We couldn't defend ourselves. They terrorised us, stinging us, sucking our blood, chewing our wings. Most of us can only walk now. We lived through some horrific hours. We were forced to empty all our hollows."

"Where are you going now?" asked Plato.

She shrugged her shoulders and more tears rolled down her face. "We don't know," she sobbed. "We're seeking refuge. We'll keep walking until we find one."

Plato spotted Wilfred sitting by the old oak tree, his head buried in his hands.

"Wilfred," he called, "we heard what happened. Aren't you going with your people?"

"No, I'm not. I've been the leader of my people for many long years and we've been happy in our old oak tree. I shall die here, Plato."

"Who are the horse flies, Wilfred? Where did they come from?" Plato asked.

"Horse flies," Wilfred replied, "are bigger than us and vicious. The females bite humans, animals and all sorts of other creatures, to get protein for bigger and healthier clusters of eggs. They lived in a cattle and horse farm some distance from here. The farmer must have sprayed the air with some kind of chemical to get rid of them and they fled here. It breaks my heart to see my people wandering like refugees to find a place to live."

"All is not lost," said Plato, patting Wilfred on the shoulder. "Where there's life there's always hope. Now, shake yourself, put some life back into your face and come with me. You must see what we have brought."

Wilfred looked puzzled. "What could you have brought us?" he said with a sigh.

Plato touched the green basket and spoke. "Here are your wounded men whom Tawny Owl our nurse has treated and brought back to life." He opened the green lid and out poured the wood flies, running in all directions and hiding in the grass. "And here" – he touched the brown basket – "is where we gathered your dead, a total waste of life because you fell for the grasshopper's atrocious scheme. Thelma has never refused kindly creatures to live in the valley and never has she spoken cruelly or insulted anyone. I would have expected better from you, Wilfred, for you've known the grasshopper's devious nature and you shouldn't have trusted him. You should have stopped Hugo."

"It was taken out of my hands, Plato. Our people backed him. They voted for his plan."

"You should have put your foot down and stopped him. You had the power as senior head."

"He got rid of me cause I was objecting to his plans. He threw me in the old people's hollow, Plato, my own son!"

Plato shook his head. Then he looked Wilfred straight in the eye and spoke in an earnest voice. "We have returned the injured wood flies, and honoured your dead. Now we want to take Thelma back to Blossom Valley."

Wilfred's jaw dropped and his voice trembled. A chilling thought seized Plato's mind.

"Hugo brought Thelma in and left her on the ground."

"She's all yours," he shouted in a loathsome voice.

I stared at him. I didn't recognise my own son. There was such fury and hatred in his eyes, I had never seen before.

"Does the body of this spider weigh as much as the bodies of our men that died?" I asked him. He shot me a hateful glare and fled. Good job too! Hugo is dead as far as I'm concerned. I thought Thelma had passed out. I kept talking to her, poking her gently on her sides, but got no response. Her body had gone cold and rigid. She was dead."

Plato gulped with shock. George let out a throaty caw and his mouth stayed open.

"Me and a few females, took her to the yew trees, not far from here. There's a thick cluster of forest daisies and we laid her down there. We covered her with leaves and twigs to keep her body safe from wild creatures, for I knew you'd come for her. I am very sorry, Plato."

The two birds turned their backs and rushed out. They searched under the twigs, parted the stems of the daisies and looked farther out, but Thelma's body wasn't to be found. Sadness clouded their faces.

"Some wild creature has already made a meal of her," George whispered and broke out in tears. "But how do we know that she wasn't beaten to death here?"

"If Wilfred says she was dead when they brought her here,

that's how it was. Wilfred doesn't lie," said Plato.

"Then it was Hugo and his men who…" George choked. "But Thelma was bold and strong, she wouldn't have given up without a fight."

"It depends how hard Hugo and his men came down on her, George."

"Did they beat her hard? Did she suffer pain?"

"Your questions cannot be answered, George. Not that it matters now." Plato said blinking back tears. "Thelma is dead!"

Both Plato and George, numbed by shock and grief, sat speechless, staring at the empty space. Then Plato shook himself up. "Let's go and tell them, George," he cried.

***

The valley grew still, wrapped in a shroud of grief and sorrow at the grave news. There was no movement, no stirring across the valley, until the third day when the burial of the dead birds was to take place.

The squirrels and rabbits dug the grave by the honeysuckle and all the bodies were laid in rows side by side. Every creature threw flowers over them and the grave was covered. Afterwards, Plato walked solemnly to the grave and placed a wreath made with glossy ivy and flaming red poppies. Everyone stood still and tearful for a minute's silence, and then they joined the ant choir in a sad farewell song accompanied by Prince Orpheo's flute.

Plato walked to the front of the gathered creatures and, looking straight across at the butterflies, spoke. "I promised to bring Thelma home alive but sadly, when George, and I got to Penny Clearing, we were told that Thelma was dead when she was taken there. We weren't able to bring her body home, for we didn't find it at the place where Wilfred had laid it nor anywhere else, we searched. So now we shall hold a service in memory of Thelma, the shrewd, but kind and caring, head of the creatures' community of Blossom Valley."

Just then, the cuckoo wheeled lazily over the assembled creatures, perched on the silver birch and started his song. "Cuckoo, cuckoo, cuckoo, cuckoo. " He paused for breath, then on and on he sang.

"He's never stayed here this long," a blackbird remarked, "and his singing isn't his usual formal sort. It's more joyful. Why isn't he leaving? Is he waiting for something? Or somebody, a fellow cuckoo perhaps?"

While the cuckoo was still cuckooing, Swift flew into the valley, circled above the trees and announced. "Thelma is on her way home. She stressed that no one is to go out to meet her, and no fuss about her return is to be made." Then Swift flew off and the cuckoo followed.

It took the creatures sometime to switch from grief to jubilation, but when gradually the unexpected sank in, they screamed and jumped and danced and cried with joy.

Twenty Three

Thelma was frail but her mind still possessed great strength and determination. She called all the creatures to a meeting. Everyone was eager and curious, for they thought Thelma would talk about her sufferings at the hands of Hugo's men, or how she'd managed to fool Wilfred into believing that she was dead when she was taken to Penny Clearing. Instead, she delivered a speech that left the creatures bewildered and gobsmacked.

"Swift told me that Penny Clearing was attacked by the horse flies. Huge numbers of wood flies were killed or maimed, amongst them children and the elderly. They're homeless. I heard they've been walking for days, searching for a new home, but to no avail. They're tired and hungry. The elderly are dying under the scorching sun. They urgently need help and we must offer it to them.

"What?" the blackbirds protested. "Feel sorry for them, after what they did to us? If they hadn't come out to invade us, they'd have been there to defend their people."

"It was one mistake a mindless young leader made." Thelma started. "He fell for the grasshopper's scam. The grasshopper got what he deserved. He was killed by his own men, and Hugo, if he's alive, will be haunted by shame and guilt all his life, which is worse than death. I urge you to get rid of the anger in your hearts and replace it with compassion for these destitute creatures. Do you agree?"

Some quiet talking went on among the birds for a few long minutes. Then the blackbird leader came forward and spoke.

"On behalf of all the birds, I say forgive and forget. You are an honourable creature, Thelma!"

"Thank you everyone," Thelma said, her voice quivering with emotion. "Up on the far western side of our valley we have three great oak trees with huge hollows. There's a stream close by and I think it'll do nicely for the wood flies."

She turned to George who was standing beside her. "Let's go and bring them to their new home, George. We shall need the ambulance cart to transport the weak, the children and the old folk. Can you tell the hares, to pick me up at the gate, George, as my legs aren't strong enough to hold me for the long walk."

***

The refugees had been walking in the hot sun without food and water and were now at the point of exhaustion. An old wood fly collapsed and a mother with two children on her back complained she couldn't walk another yard.

"We need to rest, Wilfred," the old wood fly cried. "We've been walking non- stop for hours. The children are hot and bothered. We must rest. How much farther is this copse and the creek you're taking us to?"

"I don't know," Wilfred replied with a sob. I'm not even sure we are heading in the right direction. It has been a very long time since I saw that place. I can't think straight." He broke down in tears, his body trembled and he collapsed.

A moment later a child cried out. "I can see a cart heading our way."

"It must be the creatures of Blossom Valley. They're the only creatures that have a cart," said Wilfred forcing himself to stand on his feet. "Why are they coming?"

"They're coming to wipe us out," some of the females cried. "They're only a few feet away."

The cart stopped close to the crowd that had gathered around Wilfred. A child broke away and ran to George. He had tears in his eyes.

"Are you going to kill us?" he asked.

"No, child," George replied. "We've come to help you."

Thelma walked slowly over to Wilfred.

"Thelma!" Wilfred exclaimed. "It is you… how…I am…"

"Say no more, Wilfred," Thelma interrupted. "No need to apologise. My creatures and I aren't going to hold anything against you and your people."

George looked at Thelma. "You ought to tell them," he whispered.

Thelma nodded. She slowly walked in the middle of the wood flies, and with a big smile across her face, she said. "We are here, to take you to Blossom Valley with us. A corner of our valley with oak trees and hollows and a stream close by will be your new home. You will join our community and we shall all have a happy life."

Wilfred was speechless. He tried to say something, but words wouldn't come out. The females cried with joy and the children hugged and kissed each other.

Back in Blossom Valley, the creatures came out to welcome their new friends. Plato spoke to Wilfred. "I'm glad you're here, old friend."

"I didn't want to leave my old home but the women told me they wouldn't go without their old leader. We are grateful, Plato. You're honourable creatures, all of you."

***

"Hey, George," Plato called, "now that peace has been restored and minds have eased, what do you say we go for a long flight just to refresh ourselves?"

"I say yes, Plato. Let's do it," George replied, his eyes

gleaming with excitement. Plato took him over Penny Village, over the cornfields, over Penny River and stopped at the peak of Sunrise Hill.

"I brought you here, George," he said in a calm earnest voice, "because I believe it is time that I revealed to you, the secret of the lost Kingdom of Blossom Valley. You must have wondered at times how Thelma, a spider, could be the head of Blossom Valley and why she treasured and protected the butterflies the way she did. So, here it is.

Blossom Valley, Plato started, was the oldest, greatest and the most beautiful Fairyland Kingdom in the world. Even some of the gods and goddesses of Mount Olympus came all the way from Greece to see it. They fell in love with it and almost set up home there but they were summoned back by Zeus, their great god.

Before they left, one of the goddesses gave Acacia, the Fairyland queen, a golden medallion with a big ebony stone in the middle. The gold would protect their immortality, she told her, and the ebony stone, their kingdom. The queen should wear it at all times, and each day, after the daylight dimmed, she was to touch the ebony stone and a veil would fall over the entire valley, making it invisible to the evil forces of darkness that roam over mountains and across valleys in the deep of the night.

"How come you know all this, Plato? Were you there?"

"Yes, I was, George. I have always been a close friend of Blossom Valley and what will follow, is what my very eyes saw. Please do not interrupt me again.

It was the night that Princess Estella was to become engaged to Orpheo, a prince from a faraway Kingdom. King Iolas and his Queen were busy greeting the guests who had come from different fairylands for the occasion. Dusk had already fallen, and when Queen Acacia went to touch the ebony stone, she realised she had forgotten to wear it. She rushed to her chambers, when… a distant bolt of lightning streaked down the whole length of the sky, and the mighty tearing noise of the thunder followed.

The valley shook. The trees swayed and trembled as black figures in purple robes and peaked hats riding on broomsticks, stormed the valley, growling, screaming and sniffing the air. Black smoke crackled from the tip of a wand, and a savage voice rang through the valley.

"I am the High Priestess of the Council of Tartarus. At long last, we now have your land and shall reign over it for many years to come." The High Priestess, circled the valley on her broomstick examining the surroundings. Then she raised her wand and cast her spell. "Your palace will crumble and disappear in smoke, and you, my fairy beauties of this kingdom, and all the guests, shall be turned into revolting spiders."

Almost at once the most beautiful creatures on earth became spiders, running terrified in all directions to hide.

Plato paused, his wet eyes distant, as he reached back in his mind for memories. He took a breath, then a deep long sigh, and continued.

The witches settled in, straightaway. Cauldrons frothed and bubbled, ghastly voices growled and screeched, and a vile stench filled the valley. An altar was erected in the middle of the valley, where dreadful, barbaric rites were performed. The altar was stained with the blood of squirrels, rabbits and birds that had been sacrificed, their skulls hanging on the surrounding tree branches – a chilling sight.

Some long weeks had passed when a great storm raged through the valley. Heavy rain pelted down, and fierce gusts of wind ripped trees and uprooted shrubs and bushes. Swirling masses of grass, twigs and plants, their flowers still clinging to life, were carried in torrents downhill and into the river. Amongst the masses of debris, were the bodies of the drowned spiders.

Blossom Valley had been waterlogged for some time and the witches had kept away. I flew in to see if any spiders had survived. A few came out of hiding. I couldn't tell who they were, but they knew who I was.

"I'm Thelma, Plato," one of them said. I knew Thelma had been Estella's nanny since she was born, and the queen's most trusted friend and advisor.

"Princess Estella," she said, "and a few members of the family, King Iolas, and I survived the flood. All the guests except Prince Orpheo drowned. King Iolas, is lost in his sorrowful thoughts and keeps himself in hiding. But he did tell me that his queen was not with him at that time. She'd gone to pick up the golden medallion with the ebony stone she'd forgotten to wear. He believes she is buried under the rubble. Can you please help us to find her?"

I took three moles, good friends of mine. Moles have excellent senses of smell and hearing, and spade – like paws, for digging. The torrential rain had washed tons of rubble away which made the moles' work easier. After hours of digging, they found Queen Acacia lying face down over her wand. Clasped in her hand, was the golden medallion. I took her and the surviving spiders to a safe place in the forest. After a long, anxious time, the queen recovered, and I took them back to the valley. I stayed with them.

The witches were preparing for a big celebration. An awards ceremony was to take place. The Great Wizard, master of wizards in all worlds, would award witches and priestesses for their life-time achievements.

Queen Acacia, held her wand tightly in her right hand, and taking great care, flew into a tree close by. The wizard hadn't come yet. The cauldron was bubbling, and ten witches walked round it, chanting. Black smoke coiled through the trees, and a ghastly stench filled the air. On the altar, tied by their necks, lay animals howling and crying, for they knew they were about to be slaughtered. The queen pointed the tip of her wand directly at the witches, and cast her spell.

"Evil creatures, all ten of you shall be cursed. You will be buried deep in this crater for ten long fairy years, by which time you'll have no flesh left on your bones."

A golden bolt tore through the earth and a circular crater appeared. A silver cloud lifted the ten wailing witches and hurled them deep into the crater which at once filled with water and water lilies that floated on its still surface.

She was about to cast the wish upon the spiders and Blossom Valley, when the dreadful wizard with the High Priestess riding by his side, swooped low, turned upwards and snatched the queen's wand in his raking claws. He cast his horrific spell.

"To the red mountain you shall fly and be turned to rock. I will send my hawks to peck on the rock until your flesh shows, and then…"

He hadn't finished his spell but the queen had already disappeared. The wizard still held the queen's wand in his other hand, but he didn't know that in a stranger's hand, the queen's wand had reverse and disastrous effects.

The wizard started to tremble. He dribbled revolting green stuff and fell off his stick. The priestess lifted him onto her broomstick, hid the queen's wand inside her robe and disappeared.

I followed some distance behind. The priestess took the wizard inside the Grey Caves. A minute later, I saw her run out, dribbling and shaking. She raised her hand, but before she could hurl the queen's wand away, it shot like an arrow out of her trembling grasp and travelled over the hills. I saw what I had come to see. I knew whereabouts the wand had landed. I flew back.

Thelma remembered she'd always kept a small pouch with the queen's magic dust in a secret corner of the valley. She found it and used it on the spiders, turning them into butterflies, not fairies. There was a tiny bit left and she used it on herself with the wish that she would grow big, strong and bold to keep the butterflies safe and look after Blossom Valley, until the day the spell ran its course.

"That's it George." Plato concluded with a long, exhausted sigh. "You can close your mouth now."

George blinked, in dumbstruck silence. After a while, he managed to mumble a few words. "Conti was right! The groans and cries he was hearing in his pond weren't his imagination. What will happen now, Plato?"

"Our minds were troubled enough in the last few days, George. Let us not trouble them any further. We shall know when the time comes. Now, let us fly back to Blossom Valley."

THE END

Follow the creatures' entertaining and amusing spring celebrations, emotions and gripping drama in *The Creatures of Blossom Valley* due for release next spring.

Lightning Source UK Ltd.
Milton Keynes UK
UKOW02f2357171116
287886UK00001B/10/P

9 781785 385056